the women of hearts book three

MARCI BOLDEN
STOLEN
HEARTS

Cover design by Okay Creations
Book layout by Lori Colbeck

ISBN-13: 978-1-950348-28-2

the women of hearts book three

MARCI BOLDEN
STOLEN
HEARTS

PINK SAND
PRESS

THE KNOT in Mandy's stomach tightened as she parked beneath the motel sign. Two of the letters flickered before finally going out. That seemed to be a warning. Sirens wailing in the distance were a second red flag. A voice in the back of her mind told her to drive away. Leave and never look back.

She ignored the voice and the warning signs.

She'd been promised two hundred dollars for less than an hour's worth of work. She desperately needed the money. She couldn't come up with yet another excuse to ask her brother for cash. If he found out that she'd spent her book budget—and not on books—he'd flip out. He wouldn't care that the drugs helped her sleep better than any prescription her doctor had ever given her. Over-the-counter sleep aids didn't touch her insomnia or stop the nightmares that haunted her. Her big brother had always been one of those straight-arrow types. If he found out she spent his money on pot and pills, he'd give the lecture to end all lectures. He'd also never give her another penny.

Two hundred dollars. That was all she needed now to buy her books for the semester. Then she'd be set for a few months, which would give her enough time to figure out her next move. Two hundred dollars would be enough.

Mustering up her courage, she climbed out of her car and stared at the line of numbered doors on the second floor. The man who'd answered her call told her to go to room 212.

The sky beyond the sign matched her gloomy mood. A light rain started to fall. She just hoped she could get through the modeling shoot before the clouds opened up and started to pour. She wanted to get back to her dorm before her roommate crawled into bed. They weren't on the friendliest terms as it was, but Tina got pissy when Mandy came in after ten.

Swallowing hard while she ignored the screaming in her mind, Mandy started up the flight of stairs. She had to walk on her toes because the slatted stairs tried to swallow the points of her high heels. The ad specifically said she needed to wear a short black dress and black heels. Luckily she had both. Though her shoes were scuffed, she'd done her best to cover the damage with a marker.

Peering back at the car that used to be her mother's, Mandy thought she heard Mom's voice above all the others in her head.

Go home, baby girl, she seemed to whisper.

Mandy shoved the thought away as she moved along

the second-floor balcony. How would she explain that she couldn't afford books for the next semester? How could she explain that she'd accumulated so much student loan debt before the end of her sophomore year that she couldn't get another loan without a co-signer?

She also couldn't tell her brother that her credit cards —the ones he didn't know she had—were maxed out. Nineteen and so far in debt she already didn't have a way out? No. She couldn't tell him that. Dean would never understand how she'd let this happen.

She needed this money. This would only be an hour of her life. She could do anything for an hour.

Mandy rolled her shoulders, ran her fingers over her short hair, and then knocked on the door to room 212. She prayed that the answer to all her problems was just on the other side.

Alexa Rodriguez had spent the last twelve years obsessing about the night her older sister had disappeared. Lanie had been there one minute. The next, she'd vanished. *Poof.* She was never seen again. The questions surrounding her kidnapping had never been answered. Hope that they ever would be had long ago evaporated.

Just like any traces of Lanie.

Alexa had spent so much of her teen years learning how to work missing persons cases that she hadn't considered any career other than becoming a private investigator. She didn't want to be a cop, or a federal agent, or the teacher her *abuela* had tried to convince her to become. Her grandmother preferred she do something "safe," but Alexa had been preparing for solving cases most of her life. Even so, cases like the one unfolding before her had a way of shaking her to her core.

"She wouldn't have left without telling me." Dean

Campbell had said those exact words at least four times since sitting at the table in the HEARTS Investigations conference room. "My little sister is in trouble."

"We believe you," Alexa said in a soothing tone she'd learned from her abuela.

Dean met Alexa's gaze, and the desperation in his light brown eyes broke her heart. He scowled, causing the lines around his mouth to deepen, aging him before her eyes. He was no older than thirty, but the crease between his brows had yet to ease and he had a seemingly permanent frown on his thin lips. His shaggy hair was unkempt in a way that she didn't think was usual for him. He had dragged his fingers through the brown strands enough in the last fifteen minutes for her to recognize it as a nervous habit. He was genuinely distressed. So, yes, Alexa believed that *he* believed his sister was in trouble. She'd have to confirm that before *she* believed it, but his conviction was enough for her to want to comfort him.

Holly Austin, lead investigator for HEARTS, stared at Alexa in that way she always did whenever she worried about a case hitting too close to home for one of her team-mates. Holly didn't think Alexa working missing persons cases was healthy, but at the same time, Alexa was the best one for the job.

"What do you think?" Holly asked pointedly. She wasn't asking what Alexa thought of the case. She was asking if Alexa was up for taking the case. Holly was the lead investigator for a reason. Not only because she was brilliant and strong enough to shoulder the weight, but because—whether she wanted to be or not—she was the most in tune with the others on her team.

Alexa loved that Holly always took the time to think before agreeing to take on a case. She might not be good a verbalizing how much she cared about her team, but she showed it every day in the way she looked out for them in little ways.

Dean sat across the table, his dark eyes moving from one PI to the other. "Is there a problem?"

Shaking her head, Alexa offered him a warm smile. While Holly's talent was assessing if one of her teammates was up for a case, Alexa's strength was reassuring their clients. "No. No problem. We're going to do everything we can to help you find Mandy. You'll be working directly with me, but my team will be kept informed on the case to make sure I don't overlook anything. I can't make you any promises, Dean, other than that every one of us will be dedicated to bringing your sister home."

Relief wasn't exactly the look on his face, but hope seemed to light in his eyes. "The police won't do a damn thing."

"She's nineteen, legally an adult," Alexa said. "Unless there's reason to believe she has been hurt or left against her will, there isn't much they can do."

"She might be an adult, but I still take care of her. I pay her living expenses so she can focus on school. I haven't heard from her for a *month*. She wouldn't leave without telling me. I'm her brother, for God's sake." Raking his fingers through his brown hair, he didn't notice

—or maybe he didn't care—that the strands were now standing on end. "Do you think she left against her will?"

"I'm going to find out." Opening her notebook, she scribbled Mandy's name at the top.

"We're going to ask questions, Mr. Campbell," Holly said. "Some may be personal and hard to answer, but we need you to be absolutely honest. Nothing you tell us will leave our team, and none of us are here to judge you or Mandy. Your transparency is crucial to helping us locate her. Understand?"

He nodded, but a hint of defensiveness was evident in the way he sat a little taller. That was normal. Nobody liked strangers digging into their private business.

"You said that you moved back home after your mother passed away?"

"We haven't had much contact with our dad since our parents divorced. After college, I moved to Chicago, where I was a graphic designer. When Mom got sick three years ago, I came back to take care of her. After she passed away, I moved back permanently. Mandy was still in high school, and I didn't want her to have to change schools. She was traumatized enough by losing our mom, and I can work from anywhere."

"You've checked with your father?" Alexa asked. "She's not there?"

"No. She's not there." He almost sounded angry about that. "She barely speaks to him."

"Had you and your sister fought recently?" Alexa asked.

"No. We talked at least once a week when she was at college. She seemed distracted lately, but we hadn't fought."

Alexa made a note of that fact. "Did she say why she was distracted?"

"No. I asked, but she said she had a lot going on with finals."

"Finals?" Holly creased her brow. "Didn't you say she went missing in August?"

"Yes. She went to school over the summer as well. She's determined to finish two majors in four years." Pride sounded in his voice. "She's studying journalism *and* marketing."

Alexa smiled. "She's a hard worker."

"Too hard." His proud look faded back to one of concern. "I wanted her to take the summer off, but two of the classes being offered wouldn't fit in her schedule during fall semester. She worried if she didn't take them, she would have to postpone graduation another semester. I tried to tell her that wasn't a big deal, but she wanted to finish..." He took a breath. "I said that already, didn't I?"

Alexa reassured him with another smile. "It's okay. We know you're under a lot of stress right now. Did you ever meet any of the friends she'd made at college?"

"Just her roommate and only in passing. Mandy didn't care for her too much. They didn't have real conflict that she spoke of, but she said they didn't mesh."

Alexa scribbled a note to check in with the roommate. "Was Mandy dating?"

"Not that I know of."

"Did you usually know if she was dating?" Holly asked. She lifted her hand to stop him from lashing out when he reared back, as if offended. "Some big brothers can be a little too overprotective. When that happens, little sisters keep secrets."

His face tensed. "My sister wasn't keeping secrets from me, Ms. Austin."

"She didn't mean any offense," Alexa soothed. "We just need to know how close you are with your sister."

"We talked at least once a week," he reiterated. "She never mentioned any problems or concerns. *Or* a boyfriend. She seemed to be enjoying school. The next thing I know, she's stopped answering her phone and she's stopped posting on her social media accounts. You'd think that would be enough to raise some damn red flags, but I talked to her roommate. She left school willingly. The police said she probably moved and didn't let me know because she thought I'd be mad about her leaving school. But that doesn't make sense. Yeah, I'd be frustrated and upset, but it's not like I wouldn't get over it. Something is wrong."

Alexa reached across the table and put her hand on his. "We understand. We're going to do everything we can—"

"To find her," he finished in a flat tone.

Closing her notebook, Alexa sat back. He was shutting down. She didn't blame him. He'd likely answered these same questions a hundred times while trying to convince the police his sister was in trouble. However, if he shut HEARTS out, he was going to forget something that could be vital to their case. God love Holly, but there were times her straightforward approach wasn't the best way.

"Would you take me to your house?" Alexa asked. "I'd like to take a look at her room and get a better feel for her."

"She's lived on campus the last year and a half."

"I know. But she still has a room at home, doesn't she? Seeing her space might help me figure out who she'd turn to or where she'd go."

His frown implied he didn't see the point, but he nodded his agreement. "Sure."

"Give me one minute to gather my things." Alexa pushed herself up and eyed Holly in a silent bid for her to follow.

"He's not telling us something," Holly said the moment she closed the conference room door between them and Mr. Campbell.

"I agree. I'll get it out of him."

"I don't like you going off with him—"

"He's not the bad guy, Holly." She didn't mean her words to sound so clipped, but they had. Overprotective was one way to describe Holly. She'd become more so after one of her cases had taken a bad turn and she'd gotten shot. Softening her approach, Alexa said, "I'll check in periodically."

Holly looked at the closed door, as if debating how to respond. "Keep him in your sights until you get a better feel for him. Be aware of your surroundings, Lex. I know you know this, but it's my responsibility to remind you. And take your tracker, or Rene will kick your ass. We all will."

"Yes, ma'am."

In her office, Alexa opened the top drawer of her desk. After tucking the small wallet she carried inside her back pocket, she double-checked that her Beretta sat in the holster on her hip and the personal tracker Rene, one of her teammates, insisted they all carry sat in her right front pocket.

With her phone in one hand and car keys in the other, she rejoined her new client, ready to help him find his sister.

Dean climbed out of his car and waited while Alexa parked beside him in the wide driveway. He was glad she'd agreed to take his case. He didn't doubt the other investigator's abilities, but Holly had been more pointed in her questions than Alexa. The tall brunette who had followed him home was softer. He needed that right now. He felt like shit for not knowing where Mandy was. Maybe it was selfish on his part, but he didn't need one more person making him feel like a bad brother.

"This is a lovely home, Dean." Alexa rounded the front of her black sedan, adjusting her blazer. For the first time, he realized she was carrying a gun.

Maybe if he'd taught Mandy how to handle a gun...

Shaking the thought from his head, Dean muttered his thanks before guiding Alexa to the front door. Even now, he had a hard time thinking of this as his home. He'd left for college and hadn't returned until his mother had become so ill she couldn't care for herself. This was her home. He felt like a visitor, despite having grown up here. The house looked like every other on the street. As October moved in, the grass was losing the bright green of summer and a few leaves had fallen, but the lawn was nearly immaculate.

The small porch leading to the front door didn't show signs of autumn or Halloween like the other houses. Decorations sat in labeled boxes on the shelves in the garage but hadn't been opened since his mom died three years ago. She was the one who would spend an entire afternoon digging out wooden witches and pumpkins and setting them out *just so*.

Their home had looked like something out of a decorating magazine when she was alive. He missed that sometimes. He'd never really understood her need to change everything with the season, but sometimes he did miss it.

After she died, he'd tried to keep up appearances for Mandy's sake, but once his sister went off to college, he really didn't see the point. He hadn't even put up a Christmas tree last year. Mandy's disappointment had been like a knife in his heart. She'd walked in with a smile on her face, but the moment she looked toward the corner of the living room where the tree had stood every year, her face sagged at the emptiness.

He'd justified to her, and to himself, that she was old enough now that they didn't need to do all that stuff. He'd felt guilty, though. He hadn't meant to ruin her holiday, but he had. He hadn't realized how much that tree had meant to her.

He was going to change that this year. He was determined to have her home by Christmas, and he was going to put up that damned tree and hang garland and set out all the various Santa Clauses and elves and snowmen their mother had collected over the years.

It was going to look like St. Nick himself had vomited on the Campbell house by the time he was done. He just needed Mandy to come home first.

"Dean?"

He blinked. He hadn't realized he'd stopped moving until Alexa spoke his name. Her soothing voice pulled him from his self-reflection. Swallowing, he looked around the barren porch. "I didn't decorate for Christmas last year."

Her brow creased for a moment before she seemed to catch herself and erased her automatic reaction.

"She loves Christmas. The lights and the decorations. I didn't do that for her last year. For some reason I thought she was too old. Maybe I was just too lazy." Blinking again, surprised at the surge of conflict raging inside him, he focused on unlocking the door. "Sorry. I don't know why that came out."

"Because you're worried about your sister and sometimes the brain brings up strange things when we're worried."

He swallowed, neither agreeing with nor denying her explanation. Opening the door, he gestured for her to enter first, but she gave a gesture of her own and waited for him to step inside. He did so and held the door for her. She walked in as well but didn't venture deeper into the house. She stood aside, waiting for him to close the door and drop his keys on the little table that had stood there for years. "I'm not sure what you're looking for," he said, leading her toward Mandy's room.

She followed, and though he couldn't see behind him, he suspected she was eyeing every inch they walked through, including the framed photos of three smiling faces. Alexa would probably notice that the last family photo was with their mom sitting between him and Mandy. They hadn't had another portrait taken since she'd died. No. They hadn't taken another portrait since she'd gotten sick. She didn't like having her photo taken after she'd gained weight and lost her hair from the treatment.

"Cancer," he announced.

"Excuse me?"

"My mom. Her name was Lily, and she died three years ago from cancer. You didn't ask, but you were wondering." He glanced back at her, and the curve of her lips seemed to confirm his suspicion.

"Ah. You're one of those mind-reader types."

He let a humorless chuckle leave him. "If that were the case, I wouldn't need you, would I?" He stopped in front of Mandy's bedroom door and gestured toward the space that had remained unchanged for several years.

Alexa stuck her head in, scanning the room. "I know it goes without saying that you and Mandy were devastated by your loss, but did anything about her grief unnerve you? Did she get depressed or withdraw?"

"No. Not really. Mom had been sick for a long time. Not that the length of her illness made losing her any easier," he added, as if his reasoning might be taken wrong. "I just mean that we had time to accept what was happening."

Alexa gave him another warm smile of understanding. He liked that smile. It'd been a long time since someone had tried so hard to comfort him. Most people seemed convinced that Mandy had dropped out of school to gallivant around the country or backpack across Europe or some other adventurous thing that was completely out of the norm for his sister.

Mandy wasn't the adventurous type. She was focused and studious. She had goals and worked hard to achieve them. She'd always been that way.

Leaning against the doorframe, he watched Alexa enter Mandy's room. She peered into the closet and then scanned the rest of the room as if looking for a booby trap. "Are you afraid someone's going to jump out at you?"

The slight twisting of her lips showed her amusement. "Assessing your surroundings is the first step to safety."

"And the reason you want to walk behind me?"

"Habit. Gentlemanly manners are wonderful but can also be dangerous. It's a lot easier for an assailant to get the upper hand if you don't see him coming."

Her words, even though they weren't meant to stab at him, hurt his heart, and the little smile that had toyed across his lips left.

"Sounds like common sense self-defense there," he said. "I never taught her that."

Alexa stopped looking over the room and met his gaze. "Hey, I've been trained to expect the worst in every situation. Most *people*—not just women—don't consider the potential danger of their surroundings until it's too late. Bad guys take advantage of that. Whatever is going on with Mandy is not your fault. If I had even the slightest inkling that you were responsible, I wouldn't be here right now. My hyper-awareness has nothing to do with you. I simply see the world differently than you do."

"With Mom's illness, getting Mandy through the last of her teen years fell on me. I did everything I could to make her life happy and carefree. I sent her out into the real world unprepared. You can twist that into a misguided attempt to make me feel better, but I see my *parenting* faults much more clearly now. If you tell me what you're looking for, maybe I can help."

"Did you go through her room after she disappeared?"

"A little. I thought if I could find a journal or something, I might figure out where she went."

"Any luck with that?"

"No."

She opened the top drawer of Mandy's dresser and carefully sorted through the contents. Socks and underclothes. He'd searched that already. And the next drawer she opened held pajamas, then T-shirts, and then a mix of jeans and other pants.

He didn't tell her the search was futile. He'd emptied the drawers before returning the clothing.

But then Alexa did something he hadn't. She wriggled each drawer until it came out. She examined the drawer, not the contents; then, using a little flashlight, she studied the dresser itself. She replaced the drawers and then moved on to the desk and did the same. There were only two drawers, but she went through them and the contents thoroughly.

She unmade the bed, manipulated pillows and stuffed animals, and lifted the mattress enough to peer underneath. She wouldn't find anything. He'd already done this, but he didn't stop her search. She leaned as far as she could over the nightstand, and he rolled his eyes toward the ceiling to stop the temptation of taking in the way her slacks pulled tight against her backside. However, the sound of her grunting drew his attention. Focusing on her again, he watched her stretch as far as she could to reach behind the headboard. He stepped from the doorway, closing the distance between them.

"There's a basket on the back of the headboard," she said. She climbed onto the bed and stuck her arm into the space between the wall and the carved pressed board that framed the twin-sized mattress.

When she leaned back, she pulled a small box with her. She didn't ask if he knew what was inside. It was obvious he hadn't been expecting her to find anything.

The box was long and thin, the kind that incense might come in, but when she slid the top back, there were no sticks of frankincense or sandalwood inside. Alexa pulled out a small teal-and-silver pipe. She sniffed it and then held it out to show him what she'd found.

He'd never seen that particular one, but he'd seen plenty like that when he was a teenager. Even though the pipe was hidden in her room, tucked away out of sight, Dean shook his head. "That's not Mandy's."

The look of disbelief that flashed across Alexa's face let him know how ridiculous his words had been. Of course it was Mandy's. She wouldn't have someone else's drug paraphernalia hidden behind her bed.

Rage flashed through him. Ridiculous as it was, he still refused to believe the implication of Alexa's findings. "My sister does not do drugs."

Reaching into the box again, she pulled out a small bag containing what was obviously pot. Furious, he stepped to the headboard and pulled the bed back as if it, and Alexa still perched atop, weighed nothing. There were no other drugs hidden in the basket screwed to the headboard, but there was a black and white composition book.

There it was, the journal he had searched for but couldn't find. The secrets that his baby sister had kept hidden from him. The first key to finding Mandy.

"How did you know she was hiding something?" he asked.

"Most people are hiding things, Dean." She eased off the bed and stood directly in front of him, giving him that understanding expression of hers. "Look, smoking pot doesn't take anything away from who you think she is."

"I didn't say it did."

"Your face did," she said firmly.

Sagging under the truth he knew was in her words, he shoved the bed back into place. "Medical marijuana wasn't legal here when Mom was sick. But she needed something."

"I'm not judging."

"I know that. I'm just...being transparent," he stated, reminding her that she had requested that from him. "Look at me. Mr. All-American Nerd in the flesh. Picture me searching the Internet finding a dealer." He scoffed as he recalled the first time he'd bought drugs. "I was terrified of getting caught and going to jail. What would have happened to Mandy then? Mom was dying. Mandy would have ended up living with our dear ol' dad while I sat in prison. But I did it because my mother was suffering, and that wasn't fair or right. Mom didn't like having drugs in the house either, but they did help. One night I caught Mandy in the garage smoking some of Mom's pot. I lost it. I completely overreacted. I know in the scheme of things, trying a little pot isn't a huge deal, but..." Alexa didn't seem to be condemning him or Mandy, but he still felt the need to justify his reaction. "How would you feel if you caught your little sister doing drugs?"

"I imagine it'd be frightening."

"It was terrifying. Mostly because I was the one who had brought drugs into the house."

Alexa softened her eyes. Damn her and her sweet smiles. "You weren't smoking meth in front of your sister, Dean." Putting her hand on his arm, she rubbed gently. "You did what was needed to help your mom. Kids don't always think things through. She saw her chance to try something forbidden, and the temptation was too great. Everyone gives in to the temptation to do something forbidden sometime."

Her words struck him. He didn't know why, but looking into her tender brown eyes, he had a curious moment of wondering if she meant something other than Mandy smoking pot. Shaking off the thought, he stepped back. "Do you mind if I look through her journal while you finish checking her room?"

"No. Of course not."

"I'll be in the living room if you need me." Leaving her alone, he clutched the notebook to his chest, wondering what other secrets his sister had been hiding from him.

[2]

ALEXA CHECKED in with Holly before quietly walking the rest of the rooms that lined the hallway in Dean's home. The smallest bedroom had been turned into a home office. The large monitor dominated the desk, but there was room for a calendar. She glanced over it, flipping the pages back to August, when Mandy had gone missing.

Several meetings were noted on various dates, as well as two birthdays, but nothing stood out to her. The pictures in the frames were five-by-sevens of Mandy. The images were posed by professional photographers—in one she had a volleyball resting on her hip, in another she held a clarinet, and the last was her holding a basketball in the palm of one hand. In each image, she wore corresponding uniforms in the school colors of red and black. She had been active in high school, but Alexa couldn't tell if these were taken before or after her mother's death.

The third room, the master, was obviously the most used room that she'd seen so far in the house. The queen-size bed was haphazardly made. The comforter had been pulled up, but not with much care. Clothes draped over a chair in the corner. Alexa stepped in, drawn by the photo that sat on the nightstand. Dean looked much younger in the photo as he smiled with Mandy, a tiny brunette, pulled against one side and a blonde, his mother, on the other.

Mandy was beautiful, and if the image was any indication, they'd been a normal, functioning family prior to their mother's death.

Alexa felt a pang that could only be described as jealousy. She missed her sister more than words would ever express. The fear she still felt was immeasurable. The hope, though foolish, still lingered in her mind that Lanie was out there somewhere. But if she were, the odds of her being happy and safe were minuscule. If she was still alive, she was likely living in fear and being abused in one way or another. Twelve years? No. Nothing good could have happened to her in those twelve years.

Tears bit at the backs of Alexa's eyes at the way Mandy was safely nestled against her big brother in the image. She'd probably thought nothing bad would ever happen when that photo was taken. She'd probably thought the world was a grand, adventurous place to be conquered. She probably hadn't a clue how her life was going to so cruelly teach her she was wrong.

Swallowing hard, Alexa recalled how innocent and

sweet Lanie had looked in the last picture that had been taken of her. She, too, had that same kind of naivety in her smile. The world had been hers for the taking...until *she'd* been taken.

The odds of finding Lanie now were nonexistent. But Mandy still had a chance. No, she would never be the same after whatever it was she'd gone through, but she could still come home.

"That was taken before Mom got sick."

Alexa jolted at the sound of Dean's voice. Her heart tripped over itself and dropped to her feet. Not because she'd been caught in his room—she was there to investigate his missing sister; he was literally paying her to snoop around. She was shaken because he'd sneaked up on her and she hadn't heard him. She'd been so caught up in the photo, she'd completely let her guard down while in a strange location.

Holly would strangle her if she knew.

"Your sister is lovely, Dean."

He nodded and then looked around the room. "My cleaning lady comes on Wednesday. I kind of let things go until then."

"You're going through a lot," she said, returning the picture to its place.

He grinned as she faced him. "I'd like to use that as an excuse, but I'm kind of a slob."

Smiling at his confession, she took two photos from her pocket that she'd found tucked away in the back of

Mandy's closet. The pictures looked to be taken at a night-club. The outfits Mandy and the girls with her were wearing indicated they were out partying. Alexa showed the images to Dean, and his surprise was obvious.

"Do you know these girls?" she asked.

"No." He only looked for a moment before shoving the photos back at Alexa. "I've never seen her dressed like that."

"College girls out on the town. She was with friends. I'm sure they looked out for each other."

"Do I even know her?" he whispered.

Alexa sighed. "As much as any brother can know his sister, Dean. Did you find something in the journal?"

His only answer was to look at his feet. "I'm going to make some coffee. You want some?"

"Sure." She followed him to the kitchen. Mandy's journal had been set on the counter next to a bowl that held three overly ripened bananas. "Mind if I look?"

"Go ahead."

His clipped answer said all Alexa needed to know. There was information in the pages that he hadn't known, or likely ever wanted to know, about his sister.

Easing onto one of the barstools, she opened the jour-nal. Taped to the first page was a picture of Mandy and Lily. Unlike in the image in Dean's bedroom, in this photo Lily was clearly frail. Her golden hair had been replaced by a purple scarf, and her eyes looked haunted. The dark circles under her eyes were a stark contrast to the pale skin of her face, but her smile was just as wide. Next to her, Mandy was smiling as well, but hers seemed forced. Alexa suspected her mother's illness had taken a much larger toll on her than Dean realized.

She probably hid the depth of her grief to protect her brother. From what Dean had told Alexa, Mandy seemed the type to want to protect him from any fault he might perceive in her. Not because Dean seemed unreasonably strict but because she didn't want to hurt him more than he was hurting already.

The first few pages of her neat and flowing hand-writing supported that theory. She was terrified of losing her mother. She was worried about her brother. She was taking on the weight of the world, desperate to do every-thing right to ease her family's burdens. Alexa's heart ached as she skimmed the content surrounding Lily's death. The funeral had been the hardest, based on Mandy's private thoughts. The faking smiles and reassur-ances and hearing everyone say how sorry they were for her loss had made everything so much worse for her.

The next page, her neat handwriting was askew, and her thoughts seemed jumbled and incoherent in places.

She was stoned, Alexa realized.

Mandy had added a drawing, surprisingly well done, of her mother with angel wings.

The next few pages spoke of her grief and how diffi-cult it was to watch her brother get through. Then another page of scrawled and disjointed thoughts.

Dean set a cup in front of Alexa, offering cream and sugar. She added a splash of cream and stirred as she continued analyzing Mandy's journal. The entries became fewer after she left for college, but one with an abstract drawing of a Christmas tree caught Alexa's attention. The entry, in her stoned handwriting, talked about how she needed more drugs and how she didn't have the money to pay for it. There was only one way *D* was going to give her more...

"Who is *D*?"

"I don't know."

"It sounds like they were...trading services."

"Trading services?" The muscles in his jaw tensed as he shook his head. "You can say it. It sounds like my little sister was screwing this guy in exchange for drugs."

"Well, it sounds like she was getting drugs in exchange for *something*. But she doesn't clarify what. And she also doesn't state that *D* is a man."

"Jesus Christ," he whispered harshly. "Don't turn into a Pollyanna on me. Please. I can read between the lines." Dropping onto the barstool next to her, he leaned on the counter and stared into his mug. "She was doing more than smoking pot, wasn't she? She was...shooting up or taking pills or something." He looked at Alexa with that same desperation in his eyes he'd shown at the HEARTS office. His world was crashing down around him, and he didn't know what to do or where to turn.

Alexa wanted to hug him, surround him with as much

support as she could offer, but that was definitely crossing the line of acting as an investigator. She was too soft sometimes. She knew that. That was her best trait and her worst curse. She definitely offered a softer side to her team, but sometimes she felt weak for it.

Setting her coffee aside, she asked, "Did she display signs of depression? I don't mean mourning the loss of her mother. I mean clinical depression."

"Like?"

She gestured to the journal. "It's clear she feels guilty over things completely out of her control. She writes at length about not being able to make things easier for you and your mom, but did you ever sense this was out of proportion with the normal stages of grief?"

"She always felt like it was her responsibility to take care of us. Even as a little girl she acted like it was her job to be the parent. I don't know how many times I told her she wasn't my mother."

"Did she struggle with concentration or making decisions?"

He thought for some time. "I guess sometimes. But over small things, like what clothes to wear or what to eat. She jumped into making big decisions."

"How was her sleeping?"

"She's never slept well. That used to worry Mom, but I just thought..." Running his hand over his hair, he looked around the kitchen. "I would have noticed, wouldn't I? If something were wrong?"

"Not necessarily, no. We tend to dismiss things that

we don't really want to see. And I don't just mean you or your mom. Mandy may not have even realized the struggle she seemed to be having."

"Drinking, drugs, partying. This doesn't seem like my sister."

"I'm sorry."

Meeting her gaze, he scoffed. "You know, the cops, they kept telling me she probably just went off to see the world and didn't want to disappoint me. I told them she would never do that. I told them how I know my sister, and they just...they pacified me until I wanted to punch them all. But they were right, weren't they? I don't know her. I don't know what she would or wouldn't do. What kind of brother am I, Alexa?"

At that, she had no choice but to cross that boundary of professionalism. This man was suffering, and Alexa's need to make him better was undeniable. Leaning closer, she ran her hand over his back. "You are a wonderful brother, Dean."

"You don't know that."

"I know that because I can see in your eyes how scared you are. If you weren't an amazing brother, you would find a way to dismiss her disappearance like everyone else has. You feel it, don't you? Deep in your gut, you know she needs you."

He covered his face, digging his fingertips into his forehead, and she suspected he was trying to stop his emotions and fears from bubbling over.

"We're going to find her," Alexa whispered.

That did him in. A quiet sound choked up out of his throat, and he looked at her with confusion in his eyes. "How could I not know she was using drugs?"

"Dean, people hide things all the time."

"She was..." He tripped on the words. "She was whoring herself out for drugs."

"You don't know that for certain."

"Her fucking journal—"

"Implies some things but doesn't say it explicitly. We could be reading this wrong. Let's concentrate on finding Mandy and getting her whatever help she needs. Whatever mess she is in or how she got there is done. We need to spend our energy on bringing her home."

He blew out a long, slow breath before nodding. "You're right. What's next? What do we do next?"

"Next you give me her roommate's name and any contact information you might have, and I go interview her."

"I should—"

"Not interfere, because even if they weren't close, you're Mandy's big brother and telling you anything may seem like ratting her out."

"Right. Yeah." Raking his fingers through his hair, he closed his eyes. "Uh, Tina something. Give me a second to remember."

Alexa's chest filled with sorrow for him as he pinched the bridge of his nose and squeezed his eyes closed.

"Perry. Tina Perry. She's a sophomore as well. I don't remember her major."

"That's okay. I'll find her. Mind if I take these things?"

"No. But"—he sat up and searched her eyes—"you'll be discreet, right? I don't want Mandy to be embarrassed when she comes back. Nobody else—"

She gently squeezed his arm. "I will never do anything to demean her. I promise."

"Thank you."

"I'm going to go interview her roommate. I want you to get some rest. You look exhausted."

"I can't sleep." He chuckled. "Maybe I should smoke her stash, huh?"

Alexa didn't mean to run her hand over his hair, but the strands were standing in a thousand different directions and she could no longer hold back the need to tame them. His eyes darted to hers, but something in his expression seemed more appreciative of her effort than surprised. "Or maybe have a beer and turn on a movie."

"Maybe. You'll call me."

She nodded. "I'll keep in touch, yes."

He gripped her hand as she dropped it from his head. "She's a good kid. She's just had a rough time since Mom died."

"I know. I'll call you." Taking the photos and the journal, Alexa left Dean to swallow all he'd learned about Mandy. Alexa wasn't surprised, not really. No one was as picture-perfect as Mandy so desperately portrayed herself to be. She didn't blame Dean for not seeing through the façade. Family rarely did.

In the car, she used her hands-free speaker to dial the HEARTS office.

"Hey, gorgeous," Samantha, the receptionist, answered. "How's it going?"

Backing out of the short driveway, Alexa filled her in as much as was necessary to keep her team in the loop. Sam might have been the one asking, but she would relay the information to Holly.

"I need to question her roommate. I'm headed to the college campus now. It'll take me about an hour and a half. Think you can have her photo, schedule, and dorm number for me by then?"

"And everything else you could ever need to know," Sam stated. She was constantly improving her sleuthing skills and had proven herself a real asset to the team.

Alexa was increasingly grateful for that. Sam was sweet, but she didn't always take her job as seriously as she should. She had a lot of room to grow, but with a little guidance from Alexa and a lot of patience from Holly, she was filling the role they had hired her to fill.

Turning up the radio, Alexa did her best to tune out everything. She wasn't going to start jumping to assumptions about Mandy's situation yet. Nor was she going to try to see parallels to Lanie's. Her sister had also been nineteen when she'd disappeared. She wasn't in college, though. Alexa's *mami* couldn't afford that. Lanie had disappeared while walking home from her job at a local diner. She'd waved at the cook as she left. That was the last time anyone had seen her.

Alexa had woken up the next morning to a flurry of activity. Her mother sat on the sofa crying as a police officer tried to reassure her. Her grandmother was cooking and making coffee. The neighbors were translating as much as they could. Mami and Abuela didn't speak English well, and trying to explain to the police officer that Lanie wouldn't have just disappeared was nearly impossible when Mami was crying hysterically.

Alexa had tossed on jeans and a T-shirt and rushed out to the living room. Her mother had hugged her so tight she couldn't breathe and in a mix of Spanish and English explained that Lanie hadn't come home.

Just as in Dean's experience, the police officer had said that maybe she'd run off with her boyfriend or caught a bus to start a new life somewhere else. Nobody who knew Lanie believed that. But the police didn't believe otherwise. They had searched for her, or at least listed her as missing. She'd never been found.

Though Lanie and Alexa had been born in America, Alexa got the distinct impression the police officer wasn't overly invested in finding the missing daughter of an immigrant. She'd heard him mutter under his breath that if Mami could speak English maybe he'd have better luck.

"I speak English," Alexa had snapped at him. "I'm American. So is my sister."

He'd dismissed her with a disinterested look before making more notes in his little book and leaving her mother and grandmother scared, crying, and feeling hopeless.

That was the moment that had changed Alexa. The very moment that she still recalled so clearly, the moment she'd realized it was up to her to find Lanie. She'd worked her ass off to learn the ins and outs of finding missing persons. She never had found her sister, but she hadn't given up. And she wouldn't give up on finding Mandy Campbell, either.

By the time she arrived at the campus, Sam had delivered on her promise. Checking the e-mail on her phone, Alexa found everything she needed to help her locate Tina Perry, including a map of the campus. She was standing outside a lecture hall when a mob of twenty-somethings started scurrying like roaches in a house fire. Alexa looked at the photo of Tina one more time before approaching a young woman.

"Tina Perry?"

The woman stopped and turned. "Yeah?"

"My name is Alexa Rodriguez. I'm helping Dean Campbell try to locate Mandy. Mind if I ask you a few questions?"

Tina frowned. "I guess, but my next class is right now. You have until we get upstairs."

Moving to walk beside her, Alexa started peppering her with questions. "What do you think was going on with Mandy?"

"We didn't talk much. She was popping pills and drinking. I didn't want to get caught up in that shit. I'd put in a request for a new roommate, but since it was summer semester, the options were limited. Before the school had time to resolve the issue, she dropped out."

"Do you know why?"

Starting up the stairs, Tina glanced at Alexa. "If I had to guess, I'd say either her boyfriend made her or she's too high to give a shit anymore."

"So her drug use was bad?"

"She certainly had issues. I think that jerk she was dating was the cause of most of them. When she wasn't stoned, she seemed like a sweet girl. One night I woke up to the sound of her crying. Since I'm not a complete asshole, I asked her what was going on. She told me about her mom dying and how disappointed her brother would be if he knew how much she was struggling. I told her if she wanted counseling, I'd help her. The campus has resources. She was all on board, but the next day, she came back to our room and said to forget it. Darrin, this shit stain she's been dating, wouldn't hear of it. She dropped out the next week. I don't know for certain, but I'd say he was controlling and probably a little abusive."

Darrin. Maybe he was the *D* in the journal. "Do you know how to reach her or Darrin?"

"No."

"Do you know his last name? Is he a student here?"

"No and no. I never saw him, but from what she said, it sounds like he's older. A *lot* older."

"Did you ever meet Darrin or see a picture?"

Stopping in front of a classroom, Tina shifted the bag strap on her shoulder. "No. Because I made it a point not to. I don't know what Mandy was into, but I'm pretty sure she was in over her head. Maybe I am an asshole for not trying to help her sooner, but...I got my own problems, you know?"

Alexa nodded. "I know. Whatever trouble she's in wasn't your responsibility. I get that."

"I'm sorry her family is going through this, but I'm not surprised. If they do find her, she needs rehab. Big time."

"Noted. Would it be okay if I contact you if I have further questions?" Alexa lifted her hand as if swearing an oath when Tina visibly shrank back. "I'm not going to get you mixed up in anything. I promise. Your name will never come up. I'm just trying to find her to get her the help she needs."

Tina rattled off her phone number and accepted Alexa's business card. Leaving her to continue her education, Alexa pulled her phone from her pocket. She wanted to check in with her abuela to find out what was for dinner and if there was enough to spare.

She had some bad news to break to Dean, and she'd learned that task came easier to her when she was simultaneously offering up some of her grandmother's home cooking.

DEAN INHALED DEEPLY AS ALEXA LIFTED THE TOP OFF a dish. The scents that filled him instantly made him hungry. Garlic, onion, chilies...oh, man. Heaven. "What is that?"

"Red pork posole."

He tore his gaze from the food to her, letting her know by the confusion on his face that he didn't know what that was.

She stopped unwrapping tortillas and grinned. "Pork stew with just enough spice to warm your soul. My grandmother is the world's best chef. That's not me gloating. It's a fact."

"I believe you."

"Bowls? Just point me in the right direction," she said when he started to stand.

He gestured toward a cabinet and watched as she moved around the kitchen. Something about this seemed right. She was chattering about her grandmother's cooking, about her selling tamales online and expanding into other dishes, but he was too distracted by her movements to really hear her.

When he'd left Chicago to come back and care for his mom and sister several years back, he'd left a budding relationship as well. They'd promised to try the long-distance thing, but between running his mom to chemotherapy and helping raise Mandy, as well as keep his client base growing so he had income, the relationship had taken a back seat and gradually fallen apart. After his mom died and Mandy went off to school, his habit of long days in front of a monitor hadn't changed.

He hadn't been pampered in some time. Even if it was

strictly platonic, he was going to take a few moments to enjoy this.

Alexa filled two bowls, popped the top off a container with some onions inside, and asked if he wanted any. He nodded, and she went about her business of serving him. Then she turned on the burner, tossed a flour tortilla on the flame, and flipped it before it charred, still talking about her grandmother's cooking. He couldn't help but smile at the way she accented words here and there with what he assumed was her native Spanish.

She carried a plate of several reheated tortillas to the counter. "Do you want to eat here or at the table?"

"Here is fine," he said and then regretted it. He'd thought he'd actually like to sit at the table with her. He hadn't sat at the table for a meal since the last time Mandy was home. He didn't announce his change of mind, however. He suspected he'd have another chance to sit at his table over a meal like this. Alexa was clearly used to bringing food to her clients.

For some reason that realization tweaked him a little. As special as this was for him, she did this all the time. That didn't feel right to him. He wanted this to be special to her, too, but he couldn't explain why.

He'd met the woman all of five hours ago. He hardly had any claim on her comforting ways. But for some reason, he needed to clarify. "Do you always bring food to clients?"

"Not always."

"Why tonight?"

She settled on the stool beside him. "Because you needed me to."

"I did?"

She nodded with enough confidence that he believed her, too. "You seem to be carrying this burden on your own."

"My dad agrees with the police. He thinks she got fed up with the pressure and ran off and that she'll come home soon."

"Why would he think that?"

"I don't know." He looked at her, and there was a hint of suspicion in her eyes. "You think he wasn't telling me something?"

"Maybe. Mind if I talk to him?"

"No. I'll get you his number."

"Good." She dug into her dinner.

He watched her take a delicate sip of the broth, apparently testing the temperature before taking a larger bite. "You plan on telling me what you found out from Mandy's roommate?"

She hesitated. That wasn't a good sign. Dean didn't have to be some kind of investigator to know that. He was a graphic designer. He'd learned to read his clients' body language fairly well. Too many times there was something about his work they didn't like and hesitated in telling him, as if they might hurt his feelings. Alexa had that same pause as she tore at her tortilla.

"Nothing good, I guess," he said quietly.

Alexa offered him a sad smile. "Her roommate says

she was pretty heavy into drinking and drugs. She was dating a man named Darrin, maybe the *D* in her journal. Tina said he was bad news, so that makes sense. She said he was older, not a student, and..."

"And?"

She gave him that damn sorrowful look again. "And he seemed to be very controlling over Mandy."

Anger shot through Dean. "Abusive?"

"Controlling was the word she used. She did say that she had convinced Mandy to get counseling, but the next day Mandy dismissed the idea. Tina seemed to think that was Darrin's influence."

Shoving aside his untouched dinner, Dean exhaled loudly. "I'll kill him."

"We don't know his role in this. He could be taking care of her."

"Her journal said *D* was giving her drugs in exchange for—"

"Things that we can only guess at without Mandy explaining them. Don't look for trouble where there may not be any."

He stared at her. She couldn't possibly be that naive. In her line of work, she had to have seen a hundred cases like this. Men who took advantage of troubled girls. Why was she defending this sleazeball?

"Dean."

He didn't know how she did it, but the sound of his name on her lips was so soothing. Instantly, his muscles relaxed as the word rolled through him and he forgave the irritation her denial had caused.

"I know you're scared for her. I know you're upset about the things you're learning. But let's get all the facts before jumping to conclusions. Let's look at this from every angle so we don't miss something. We need to figure out who this Darrin person is and what role he has played, if any, before we crucify him."

He closed his eyes. Logically she was right, but that didn't make him not want to beat the hell out of this unknown man anyway.

"I need you to prepare yourself for something," she said in that melodic tone that eased his mind.

Focusing on her again, he took a breath to brace himself for whatever she was about to toss his way.

"You're right when you say Mandy is in trouble. We don't know what that trouble is or how deep it runs. What we do know is that she seems to have a substance-abuse issue and a codependency on this man. When we find her —and I say when because I believe we will—there is a likelihood that she will be blinded by her addiction. She's probably not going to be thinking clearly. She's going to associate you with all the stressors that got her to this point. She's probably going to be angry and lash out at you. She might even want to stay with whoever is helping her because he's likely to have convinced her that she needs him and that he's the only one she can count on. She's going to resist your help, and because she's an adult, she has that right."

"I'm not going to leave her—"

"I'm not saying you should or that we will. I'm trying to prepare you for what you may face when we find her. This may not end with just finding her. You may have to fight her every step of the way to get her the help she needs. Even then, Dean, no matter how hard you try, she may choose to never come home. Do you understand?"

He sank back on the barstool. He hadn't considered that. He'd been so determined to find Mandy and help her that he hadn't considered she might not want his help. "How do I... What if..."

She put her hand on his, and he automatically squeezed her fingers, needing her support. "Start looking for a family attorney now. Someone who can help you try to get guardianship over her and force her into rehab if it comes to that. You may not need to, but you should start preparing for that so you aren't scrambling once we find her. If you aren't sure where to start, we can meet with Tika, one of my teammates. She's our legal expert. She can help point you in the right direction."

Dean's heart and spirits sank with every word she said. By the time she finished, he felt like the world had been yanked out from beneath him. "How did we get here?" he whispered, not really speaking to Alexa. Obviously she didn't know, couldn't know. But he didn't know, either.

She stepped off her stool and wrapped her arms around him. "I'm sorry," she whispered. "I'm so sorry."

Dean hadn't expected her embrace, nor had he realized how much he needed it. With her arms around him and her heat warming him, he suddenly didn't feel quite so alone in his fears. Slipping his arms around her waist, he pulled her to him and soaked in the comfort she was offering, not caring that she was a virtual stranger. Right now, she was the only chance he had at finding his sister, and if she were willing to shoulder some of his stress, he'd gladly let her.

[3]

ALEXA SKIMMED the long list of usernames Mandy had accumulated for her social media accounts. While most of Mandy's friends were still in "circling the wagons" mode, determined to protect and preserve their friend's privacy and dignity, Alexa had convinced one to cough up links to all the websites where Mandy posted pictures and status updates. She wasn't focused on researching Mandy's activity right now. She needed to find this Darrin person and determine if he had been supplying Mandy with drugs.

As soon as she found him and figured out his full name, she might be able to pinpoint his location and hopefully find Mandy in the process.

Mandy's social media was pretty much what Alexa expected. A facade. A show of how great college life was. She did notice, however, that the posts had changed over the last year. Mandy's freshman year was filled with photos of her at activities, participating in events. By the end of her first year, those images changed to selfies of the girl with heavy makeup, hair done, lips pouted. Eyes glazed.

Alexa didn't blame Mandy's online friends for not noticing the difference. These images weren't anything new to the social media platform. These photos were just a few of hundreds on someone's feed. Alexa noticed because she was looking. Really looking. Something had shifted dramatically about a year prior to Mandy's disappearance.

Alexa didn't have to think too hard about what that could be.

On her own for the first time in her life with a growing addiction? Mandy had likely managed to balance those two things the first few months, but eventually, as tended to happen, the addiction took over. A year into being without the influence of her older brother's care, Mandy had lost control of the thing she likely thought she was handling.

"Hey," came a voice from the door.

Alexa tore her gaze away from a photo of Mandy with her hair puffed out, lips painted red, and glitter on eyes lined with black.

Rene eased into the room, tilting her head as if afraid she might be interrupting something. "What are you thinking?"

"Nothing I can prove yet."

"Such as?"

"It's not uncommon for young women who get caught

up in drugs to get caught up in other things to keep in supply."

Rene lifted her brows. "You think the Campbell girl is a sex worker?"

"I think she got in over her head and there are always people willing to offer drug addicts in over their head an alternate solution."

"I hope you're wrong."

"Me too." She turned her monitor to show Rene the image. "About a year ago, her posts went from innocent to...possibly not so innocent. Seemingly overnight."

"Could be that guy she was dating."

Alexa nodded. "Or it could be a young woman trying out a new style. Anything is possible. Including me reading too much into these photos."

"What does your gut say?"

"My gut says someone saw she was in trouble and instead of throwing her a lifeline, they threw her an anchor. She's out there somewhere drowning, and if I don't find her—"

"We can't save everyone," Rene stated firmly. That was the reminder they had to give each other on a regular basis. Every one of their team seemed to take on more burden than they should, more responsibility for their clients than was reasonable. Drawing the line between investigator and human wasn't always as black and white as it should have been. Sometimes cases drew them in and consumed them.

Alexa started to tell Rene she was aware of that, but

then she stopped and smiled. "You guys are worried about me?"

"Always."

"I appreciate that, but I'm doing fine. Really. I'm worried for her. For her brother if...if we don't find her or what he'll learn if we do. But I'm fine."

"I know how cases of missing young women stir memories for you. If you want help on this case, let me know, okay?"

"I will."

Alexa returned her attention to Mandy's social page and her original mission of identifying Darrin and determining whether he was the mysterious *D* mentioned in Mandy's journal. After skimming a year's worth of images, she moved on to other social media sites, where she stopped scrolling when she reached the previous Christmas.

A photo of Mandy and Dean caught her eye and mesmerized Alexa for some reason. They were pressed cheek to cheek, and the smiles on both were...content. To anyone else, their smiles might have seemed bright and heartfelt, but Alexa saw more in their eyes than the eerily similar amber hue they shared.

Sadness undercut the joy they were exuding. Their first Christmas without their mother. Bittersweet time between siblings. Early enough into Mandy's addiction that she could still hide it. Alexa tried to concentrate on the missing young woman, but her focus kept drifting back to Dean. His face was as clean-cut in the photo as in the one she'd seen in his bedroom. Before his mother had died and Mandy had gone missing.

His eyes reflected the increased burden in the photo on Alexa's screen, but nothing like what she saw in them when he gave her that pleading look that seemed to be fixed to his face. His eyes held her captive now that she didn't have to worry about him noticing her stare. A slight hook to his nearly perfect nose pointed to full lips that spread wide with his smile. His teeth, like his nose, had just enough imperfection to add to his appeal.

Perfect...but not quite.

Handsome enough to know it, but not conceited enough to take it to the next step. She liked that. She liked his strength, physically and emotionally. She liked the confidence he seemed to harbor in these older photos, the ones before his life crashed down on him a second time. More than anything, she liked how much love he clearly had for Mandy.

She's in trouble, she heard him say in her mind. *My little sister is in trouble.*

"Yes, she is," Alexa whispered to his photograph. She just hoped she was able to find Mandy and convince her to get the help she so obviously needed.

Deciding she needed caffeine to get through the rest of Mandy's social media, Alexa headed toward the little break room where the team drank too much coffee and shared snacks, and where someone—Eva, she suspected—kept a bottle of vodka in the freezer.

"Don't put that away," she said when she walked in

just as Holly was about to return the coffee carafe to the burner.

Holly glanced over her shoulder as she grabbed another mug and filled it. "How are things going?"

"I'm growing more and more confident she has been pulled into prostitution and..." She let her words trail off when she realized Holly wasn't actually listening to her. Nudging the team leader with her elbow, she waited until they made eye contact.

Holly's almost clear blue eyes seemed haunted. Whatever was occupying her mind was not a happy thought.

Putting her hand to Holly's arm, she squeezed lightly. "Hey. What's wrong?"

"Nothing."

Alexa frowned dramatically to show her disbelief. "Bullshit."

Holly shook her head as if to dismiss the conversation, but Alexa wasn't so easily discouraged. Of all the women around here, she was the only one who seemed comfortable talking about things, which explained why her teammates tended to open up to her more easily. Holly tugged on the silver heart charm that dangled from her necklace, a sure sign she was anxious about something.

The pendant had belonged to her mother. Alexa had never seen Holly without it. She'd asked about it one night while the two of them were out drinking away a case gone bad. Holly had shared that when she was eight years old, she'd witnessed her mother's rape and murder. Alexa tried to get her to talk about it more than once, but Holly always shut down.

"How do you ever get any work done?" Holly asked. "When I walked by your office earlier, you were in a therapy session with Rene. Now me?"

Alexa grinned. "It's not therapy, Hol. It's friendship. Friends talk." Tilting her head, she whispered, "Is it about your mother?"

The jolt that shook her seemed to indicate Alexa had hit the issue right on the head.

Holly started to protest, but something in her eyes seemed to give in. "I told you I've been trying to find the man who..."

"I know."

"It's a long shot. My mom was murdered over twenty years ago. Finding her killer now..."

Alexa's stomach tensed. The uneasiness in Holly's voice was something she'd never heard before. Holly was always so damned confident.

"What did you find?" Alexa pressed.

Holly licked her lip and stared into her mug. "I never told my dad that I was researching Mom's death. Jack thought it was important to question him, since he found her."

"Yes, I know."

When an intruder had kicked in the back door while Holly and her mother were watching television, her mother had hidden Holly. Then, just a little girl, Holly had peered under the couch and witnessed her mother's assault just before she was stabbed to death. Though Holly still believed she froze, anyone else would understand the girl had been in shock. She had stayed hidden until her father came home from working the late shift and found the scene and finally rescued her from her hiding place.

Holly blinked, seeming to pull herself from whatever was playing out in her mind, and looked at Alexa. "He was furious. Not that we brought up bad memories, Lex, but that we were trying to solve the case. His reaction was... unsettling. To say the least."

Taking the mug Holly had filled for her, Alexa sat at the table and patted the surface until Holly joined her. Putting her hand on Holly's arm, she searched her gaze. "What are you thinking?"

"Things I don't want to think," she whispered, sounding ashamed.

"Do you think your father had something to do with the attack?"

Closing her eyes, Holly let out a slow breath. "I don't want to. If he were a witness in any other case, that would be my instinct. But he's... This is my dad, Lex. He's a drunk and an idiot and completely irresponsible. But he's still my dad, and I shouldn't be thinking that he could have had something to do with what..." She put her hand to the pendant dangling from her neck.

"Shh," Alexa soothed. "Don't let your mind go back to that night. Not right now. Holly, sometimes people we love do bad things. You know that as well as I do. But sometimes, as PIs, we look so hard for signs that people did bad things, we see things that aren't there. What does Jack think?"

"After the funeral, Dad put me in martial arts classes and taught me how to use a gun. I always told myself he did all that as his way of coping. He wasn't there to protect us when Mom was murdered, so he wanted to make sure nothing like that happened to me. That made sense in my mind. Jack thinks that Dad's reaction was more of a PTSD response. All the classes and time spent shooting was over the top. I agree with that, but I really felt that he just needed to know that if someone ever came after me, I could handle it. His reaction last night was more than that. He warned us not to get involved. That it was over, to let it go, that he wouldn't have any part in trying to solve this case." She creased her brow. "I didn't feel like he was saying any of that out of a parental concern that something might happen to me, not like I thought when I was young. He was scared, Lex. He was scared of what I might discover."

"I think it's time to pass this on to the team. Let us take over."

"No, I can't—"

Gripping Holly's hand, Alexa lifted her brows to emphasize how serious she was about what she was about to say. "If your father was somehow involved in your mother's death, you should not be the one to discover that."

"Jack is helping me."

"That's great. Jack is a wonderful detective. He's also too close to this. Let us take this over."

Holly sat quiet, but only for a few heartbeats, before shaking her head. "I owe it to my mother to find the truth. No matter how ugly it is."

"Hey, guys," Tika said hesitantly from the door. "Everything okay?"

Alexa waited, hoping Holly would tell their teammate the truth.

Holly cleared her throat and pushed herself up. "Long day already. That's all. How are you?"

"Fine," she said, clearly not believing Holly's response. She watched, a look of perplexity on her face, as Holly left.

As soon as they were alone, Alexa frowned and shook her head, signaling Tika to keep her questions to herself—she wouldn't be answering them.

Sipping her coffee, she sat back, hoping the legal mind of their team didn't need to unload. As much as Alexa enjoyed being the sounding board for her team, she was feeling a bit drained after Holly's confession.

DEAN PARKED OUTSIDE HIS DAD'S HOUSE AND STARED up at the two-story farmhouse. Years and years ago, this block used to be one big lot with horses and sheep. As time passed and progress moved into the area, the original owner was pushed out and the lot broken into several.

Even so, the original plot of land with the farmhouse had the biggest yard on the block. As a kid, Dean had begged to come to his dad's house because there was so much more room to play outside.

His mom didn't bring him and Mandy over often. She always had excuses for why they couldn't go. It wasn't until Dean was a teenager that he realized that his dad didn't want them there. He had remarried and his new wife had two kids of her own—kids who seemed to have replaced Dean and Mandy. Even their names were similar: David and Maggie.

His mom had lied to protect her kids from knowing they were unwanted by their own father. Dean remembered how frustrated it would make his mother when he asked, but she never told him the truth until he pushed the issue one day.

She'd frowned and apologized as if it was her fault she'd married a bastard.

He never understood how his father just walked out of one life and into another without any consideration for the family he left behind. He had just accepted it as fact and did his best to stop caring that he and Mandy meant less to their father than their stepsiblings, whom they barely knew. As time went on, they saw less and less of their dad and his new family.

Neither Dean nor Mandy had asked why. Neither had cared.

However, everything seemed like a lie now, seemed to be a facade, and thinking about the sudden break in his family caused a nagging in his gut that was like a tsunami warning.

Run for higher ground, a voice in his mind screamed, *before you get swept away.*

Instead of listening, he turned off the ignition and opened the car door. Huffing out a heavy breath, he forced his feet to move up the sidewalk until he was pressing on the doorbell. Looking around, Dean realized that the landscaping hadn't changed in as long as he could remember. Everything was the same. Trisha, his stepmother, made sure everything looked immaculate on the surface, but Dean knew better.

Lies, bitterness, and a whole lot of resentment were hidden within these walls.

His dad opened the door, and Dean wasn't surprised at the frown that formed on the man's lips.

"May I come in?" Dean asked.

Still scowling, his dad stepped aside. "It's late."

"It's seven."

"You should have called first."

"You wouldn't have answered."

His dad closed the door and scuffed the heels of his slippers as he crossed the living room to sit in his recliner. He hadn't used to drag his feet, but the last few years had added too much weight around his center and had likely taken a toll on his knees.

As he skimmed the room, a sense of nostalgia washed over Dean. Just like the landscaping, the interior of the house hadn't changed much.

"I haven't been here in a while," he said, more to himself than to his father.

"Because you are always too damn busy."

Dean winced, stunned at the bitter accusation. No. It was because his father and stepmother had made it clear he and Mandy weren't welcome. "Excuse me?"

With a harsh shake of his head, his dad dismissed the question. "What do you want?"

"I hired a private investigator to find Mandy since the police won't help."

"Leave the girl alone already, Dean. She's out experiencing the world. That's all."

Staring down his father, he wondered if the man was really so out of touch with how the world was changing that he wasn't at all concerned about his daughter disappearing without a trace. "Has she reached out to you?"

"No."

"Has she called you or come by lately?"

"No. Damn it." Clear agitation clipped his voice, and he exhaled harshly before pressing his lips together.

Dean and his father had always looked so similar, but seeing the way the man sagged and scowled made him silently vow to never let himself grow to look so angry and haggard. He'd add an extra set to his workout routine and toss the chocolate chip cookies that tempted him far too often. Anything to prevent himself from going down the road his father had taken. "Did she tell you she was leaving?"

Cutting his sharp gray eyes to Dean, his father said, "I

answered the police when they asked these questions. And I gave them my opinion on the matter."

"That Mandy just walked out on her life, dropped out of school, and vanished without a trace because that's what kids do."

"I did it."

Dean pointed at his father, his own frustration starting to boil to the surface. "You backpacked across the Southwest with a buddy and constantly checked in. Grandma knew where you had been and where you were headed. I heard the stories, remember?"

Narrowing his angry eyes, his dad said, "If Mandy had a mother, I'm sure she'd check in with her. Lily is gone. Mandy is an adult. She doesn't answer to you."

"I am her brother. I'm worried about her."

"Don't be. She's fine."

"How do you know?"

He waved his hand as if to dismiss Dean's concerns.

Swallowing the urge to lose his mind on the man, Dean tried for a calmer approach. "I just want to know that she's safe. I want to know that she isn't hurt. If you know that for certain, tell me."

His dad stared at him for a long, drawn-out moment that made Dean's heart start to race. "Mandy is fine. She's not hurt."

"Where is she?"

"She's fine, Dean." He nodded toward the door. "See yourself out. My show is about to start."

His show was old reruns of *Matlock*. Some TV series

from the goddamned 1980s was more important than discussing his daughter's health, security, and whereabouts.

Putting his hands on his hips, Dean pushed a breath between his lips. "One more question."

"What's that?" his dad asked, as if daring Dean to push his very last button.

"What the hell did I do to you to make you hate me so much?"

As he held his gaze, his father's eyes seemed to darken. His face hardened, and his scowl deepened. "I don't hate you, Dean. I'm just so disappointed in you I can't see straight."

His answer shook Dean, though he shouldn't have allowed it to. "Why? What did I do?"

"Get the hell out of my house."

"Dad—"

"*Get out*," he stated, emphasizing every word.

Dean hesitated, wanting to push him hard, but finally threw his hands up. "Whatever," he spat under his breath. "What the hell ever."

He stormed out of the house, slamming the door behind him, and didn't stop marching until he was inside his car. Staring up at the house, he shook his head, not understanding or believing what had just transpired.

He had no idea what his dad's problem was. No clue. But he had far too much on his plate to worry about it now. His baby sister was out there somewhere. He was going to find her.

[4]

ALEXA PREFERRED to interview people in person, but Dean's dad was being difficult. She suspected that was intentional. He didn't seem concerned about his daughter, nor did he seem interested in his son's concerns.

"Mr. Campbell," she said calmly, "I need fifteen minutes of your time. I'm willing to come to you. You can't tell me that you don't have fifteen minutes to spare to help locate your daughter."

"I am booked until the end of the week."

"Your son is very concerned about Mandy."

"Look, *Alexia*."

She closed her eyes and bit back the urge to correct him on her name for a third time.

"Lily pushed that girl too hard, and when she died, Dean picked up where she left off. Mandy burned out. Now that she's an adult and out from under his thumb, she ran off. That's it. End of story."

"I'm not doubting that, but it would ease Dean's mind greatly if he could just confirm that."

"I wish I could help you."

"Is there a reason you can't?" She tapped the tip of her pencil on her desk, waiting for his reply. "Was your ex-wife ever abusive toward Mandy?" She was confident she knew the answer to that. She had a fairly good instinct about people, and nothing about Dean's behavior indicated that his mother ever hurt him or his sister. She didn't even really believe that he or Lily had pushed Mandy too hard. Dean seemed concerned about the pressure she'd put on herself, not the other way around.

"No," he answered flatly. "Not like fisticuffs abusive. But her expectations were unrealistic. Nobody could ever live up to the image Lily painted of her little princess. Dean had it easy, being a boy. Mandy's the one Lily put on a pedestal."

The anger in his tone set Alexa on edge. "What do you mean?"

"Ever since she was a kid, Lily pushed her to try harder, be better. From band all the way through basketball. Even when she was dying, Lily pushed and pushed. Mandy had enough pressure without trying to be the perfect angel. Then Dean came home to take care of Lily, and he wouldn't lay off her. Mandy couldn't handle the pressure."

"Mandy told you this?"

"Yeah. She was home for Christmas last year and needed money. I asked why she didn't tell her brother, and she broke down. She said she couldn't handle asking him for help because he'd just tell her she needed to try harder."

"Have you ever seen him act like that toward her?"

He was silent for so long, Alexa thought he wouldn't answer, but then he said, "Look, I walked away from that mess a long time ago. Lily was crazy. Happy one day, depressed the next. We never knew what to expect from her. It got to be too much for me."

"Was she ever diagnosed as manic depressive or bipolar?"

"Hell if I know. She went crazy one day and threatened to kill me. I stormed out and never looked back."

Alexa closed her eyes. "Your wife was threatening to kill you, so you walked out and left her to care for your young children?"

"Lady, I don't know what world you live in, but Lily would have had to put me in the hospital before a judge gave me custody of those kids. It's a mother's world; fathers just live in it."

"But if you thought—"

"Are you calling to judge me or ask about Mandy?" he snapped.

She bit her lip to stop any more accusations from flying. "I apologize. What makes you think Mandy reached her limit?"

"Because she said as much the last time she came by. She said she'd had a fight with Dean and needed gas money to get back to campus. I handed her a twenty and told her to just stay gone. To leave him alone. She said she planned to."

Alexa tried to reconcile what the man was saying with the image of Dean she'd formed in her mind. "Maybe some of their stress was because Lily was ill?"

"Look, I know Dean loves his little sister. That's not what I'm saying. But he's a hardass. He always has been. With everybody. Just like Lily; no one ever lives up to his expectations. He has this way of looking at you like you're the biggest letdown he's ever known. I can't imagine Mandy having to see it all the time. I'm not saying that I like what she's done, disappearing like this. But I under-stand it. She needed a break from the pressure. That's all."

Alexa let his words roll through her head. "Do you know where Mandy is?"

"No."

"Has she contacted you?"

His drawn silence was all the answer Alexa needed.

"Mr. Campbell, Dean is terrified for his sister. If you are in contact with her, you really need to let him know that she's okay."

"Listen, she'll come back when she's ready. He just needs to leave her alone for a while."

Alexa wanted to push more, but the man hung up. She wasn't going to get much more out of him unless she had a different approach, and she wasn't about to betray Dean's trust and spout off about Mandy's drug use. She would, however, lean on Dean a bit harder. There was more to the story. If Lily really had been suffering from some kind of disorder that was bad enough to end her marriage, then it certainly impacted her children as well.

Mandy might be having some kind of breakdown, which could drastically change the way Alexa approached this case.

She didn't doubt Dean's sincerity in his concerns for his sister, and she had believed him when he said he thought Mandy pushed herself too hard, but she also needed to get to the bottom of his father's accusations.

"Knock, knock," came a voice from the door.

Alexa smiled at Rene. Before Holly had gotten shot working a case a few months prior, Rene had been the most paranoid on the team. She'd lost her partner in a shooting when she worked as a federal agent, making her more aware than some of how badly cases could go.

"How's the case going?" Rene asked, walking in.

Rubbing her temple, Alexa growled out her frustration. "I get the impression her father knows where she is but isn't willing to help me find her because he thinks Dean is too tough on her. But the father also told me Dean's mother suffered from some kind of mood disorder that was bad enough for him to walk out on her. Which makes me wonder if his sister could have the same disorder. Whatever it was. And now I have to ask Dean about this." She frowned as she shook her head. "I don't think he's going to appreciate that. The guy is so close to losing his mind with worry. I'm a little concerned what he'll do if he thinks his dad is holding out on him."

"You're so much more human than the rest of us. How do you do that?"

Alexa chuckled as she used an elastic band to tie her long hair back. "My grandmother is my saving grace. Every night she reminds me how important it is to remember why I do this."

"You're lucky to have family."

The sadness in Rene's eyes caught Alexa off guard. Rene's parents had died when she was in her twenties. As an only child, she'd been on her own most of her life. She said that was why she was so hardened, but everyone at HEARTS knew there was a darker story in Rene's past. She was just so good at hiding it, no one had ever really pressed. They all had things in the past they only shared when they chose.

Holly's mother had died years before—although not all of the HEARTS knew the specific circumstances, and they didn't ask. Eva had faced years of sexual harassment from her superiors and peers before leaving the police force. Alexa's sister had been kidnapped and never found. Rene...well, her real story was still to come. Tika had dropped out of law school after facing unexpected discrimination from not only her peers but her instructors as well. The offenders were never charged because the school had found her account of their threats and harassment "unreliable." Sam was tired of not being taken seriously, but she was correcting her course and working on growing up and earning the respect of the team.

They all had pasts and secrets. That was part of what

bound them so tightly together. Their scars and pain and stories of survival—even if they hadn't all revealed those scars and pain and stories—made them stronger as a team.

"Hey," Alexa said with firm tenderness. "We're your family. Me and the rest of the HEARTS."

"You know what I mean," Rene said, letting her edgy New York accent come through.

Alexa's concern continued to grow. Not only was it unlike Rene to show emotion of any kind, but she was always cognizant of her accent and did her best to keep her voice neutral. She said too many people stigmatized her natural inflection. They considered her either ignorant, or more often, a mobster, since her olive skin and dark brown hair were stereotypical of her Italian roots. Rarely did anyone see beyond her accent to the authority figure she tried to portray. Hearing her speak with the choppy tone took Alexa by surprise.

"What's up, Rene?"

She shrugged. "Nothing."

"Bullshit," Alexa snapped.

The corner of Rene's mouth lifted. "You're adorable when you cuss."

Alexa faked a wide smile. "Well, you're adorable all the time, but don't change the subject. What's wrong?"

Stress played across Rene's face, creasing her brow and turning her half smile into a deep frown. "I just wanted to check in. I know missing persons cases can stir some bad memories for you."

Alexa felt the pain of the past stab through her heart.

"The difference is that my sister didn't get caught up in drugs and destroy her life. She was taken off the street."

"I'm sorry to bring it up."

"Don't be. I think about her every day," Alexa admitted, unable to stop her eyes from darting to the picture of her and Lanie.

Sam rushed into Alexa's office with a small stack of papers, disrupting their conversation. "I got her credit report. Mandy Campbell has some serious debt. You can blame most of that on the high-interest credit cards." She stopped, seemingly aware that she'd interrupted something. "Um, I can come back."

Rene stood. "No. This is much more important."

Alexa opened her mouth to debate that, but Rene was gone before she could. She decided she'd follow up on that later; for now, she wanted to see what Sam had found. Taking the papers, she let out a low whistle. "She is way too young to have a credit rating that trashed."

Sinking into the chair Rene had just vacated, Sam sat forward. "Is she okay? She's seemed off lately."

Alexa loved Sam, adored her spunk, but she didn't care for how blatantly nosy the woman was being at the moment. Her ability to search the Dark Web was constantly improving and making her invaluable to the team, which made Alexa happy because more than once she'd gone to bat for Sam with Holly. Holly didn't think Sam fit, but Alexa knew she just needed time to find her place, which she had. She was just as much a part of the team as any of the investigators, but right now, her question felt like she was trying to shove her way into Alexa's tight bond with Rene.

Alexa shook her head. "Don't worry about it."

"Is she okay?"

"Yeah. She's fine," Alexa said, but she suspected otherwise.

Sam sighed audibly. "You guys never tell me anything."

Alexa tilted her head and said, "Because you hold secrets about as well as a strainer holds water."

Sam playfully glared before saying, "Not true. I haven't told a single one of you that Jack is planning to propose to Holly tomorrow night." Sam sank back in her chair, screwing her face up as she realized what she'd just said. "Damn it."

Alexa's mouth gaped, and her eyes widened. "Do not say another word until you close that door."

Sam jumped up, eased the door shut, and then plopped back into her chair. "Okay, get this," she said with the girlish excitement of a high schooler. "He called me yesterday and asked me to make sure everyone stays for the Friday dinner. I reminded him that now that Eva and Josh are back together, we always do because Josh brings in a big dinner. Friday dinner is like our little family tradition again, right? He's like, 'yes, I know, that's why I want to make sure *everyone* is there.'"

Alexa giggled at the way Sam slipped back into her habit of gossiping like a hen. She'd been trying to watch herself. Holly didn't care for gossip, since client confidentiality was crucial to their business, and the way Sam excitedly shared everyone else's business hadn't done her any favors when she'd started working with HEARTS. She had really restrained her tendency to gab about the latest breakups, marriages, and Hollywood affairs, but seeing her now was just like old times.

"Anyway," Sam continued without seeming to take a breath, "I was like, 'Jack, what's the deal. Why are you so stressed out?' *And he said*"—she drew out the last few words—"'I'm going to surprise Holly with a present, and I just want to make sure everyone is there to see it.' I knew right then, the way he said it. So I asked if that's what he was going to do. He tried to deny it." She sat a bit higher. "But I used some of the new interrogation skills I've learned to pry the truth out of him. Of course, he then threatened me with my life if I told anyone, so you damn well better act surprised."

Alexa nearly exploded with excitement. "Oh my God. Holly is going to freak."

"I'm not sure that's a good thing." Sam tapped her pink-painted lip with the tip of her manicured nail. "She's so private, Lex. I don't think she's going to appreciate having everyone here to see her reaction."

Alexa shook her head. "No way. She may play like she's tough as steel, but she loves Jack. We are family, and Holly would want her family to share in this. Speaking of which, did Jack invite her father?"

"I don't know. But Jack is bringing Najwa."

Jack's mother was an angel determined to have grandchildren. She'd been pushing for Jack to wed Holly before they'd even settled into dating. Now that he was proposing, it probably wouldn't be long before they did have kids. A real family. Alexa didn't want to feel jealous of her friend, but there was that nagging in the back of her mind again.

Sam sighed wistfully, pulling Alexa out of her spiraling thoughts. "I hope she says yes."

"She will. She's crazy for Jack."

Rubbing her palms together, Sam bit her lips, but the excitement inside her bubbled out. "I'm going to help her plan. I don't care what she says. She's not running to the courthouse or having some simple ceremony. She's not treating her wedding like just another thing. We're blowing this bitch out. Holly is getting married. I can't believe it."

Alexa chuckled at Sam's determination, but that same internal disappointment at her own lack of success in the romance department flared at the idea of Holly's wedding. "Well, good luck with that. I'll help however I can."

Sam didn't seem to notice the slight dip in Alexa's enthusiasm as she asked, "Think I should I get a cake? Would that be too much? For Friday, I mean. Not for the wedding. Obviously we'll have a wedding cake."

"Yeah," Alexa said. "That'd be good. Don't pick it up until after lunch, though. You can't hide a cake around here all day. Somebody will sniff it out and wonder why you have it."

The wheels were obviously turning in Sam's mind.

"Awesome." She stood and started for the door but then stopped. "Hey, how's your client holding up?"

"Not well," Alexa said without the conspiratorial tone she'd had moments before. "I'm worried, actually. I think he's taking a lot of blame that isn't his. Have you had any luck finding signs of Mandy online?"

"Not yet. All her social media accounts are still active, but she hasn't posted since leaving."

Alexa put voice to something she had been hoping to avoid. "Do you have time to start searching for her photo on sex sites?"

"You want me to search the Dark Web? Because I honed those skills with Eva's last case. It's a little frightening how good I am at finding sex videos."

Eva's last case had been a crazy mix of peeping tom meets *Stepford Wives* meets revenge porn. Alexa still couldn't quite wrap her mind around it, but it added another layer of services for HEARTS. On top of investigations and self-defense basics for women, they'd added a monthly class on how to identify hidden cameras. The fact that those types of classes were needed pissed her off, but that was the world they lived in. The least they could do was share some of their knowledge to those who might benefit from it.

"I don't think she's making movies. If anything, she's being trafficked. Check escort sites," she clarified for Sam. "Black listings that sell sex. That sort of thing. There's a document on our cloud drive with a list of sites I'm aware of, but look around. New sites pop up all the time."

Sam's eagerness faded. "Yuck."

"If you aren't up for it—"

"I am. I can do it. If she's out there for sale, I'll find her."

"Thanks. Sam?"

"Yeah."

"I'll staple your damn lips shut if you tell anyone else Jack's secret."

She pretended to zip her lips and toss away the key, but Alexa knew better. By the time Jack presented a ring to Holly, almost everyone at HEARTS would know what was coming.

DEAN HADN'T EXPECTED TO SEE ALEXA FOR LUNCH, but he was glad she'd stopped by. After he let her in, he saved the design project he had been working on while she reheated some of the posole from the night before. When he entered his kitchen, the scent of garlic and chili peppers filled the air as Alexa reheated tortillas over the open flame as she had the night before. Something about her fluid movements entranced him. Or maybe it was the lack of rest he'd gotten for the last few months.

"Smells delicious," he said by way of announcing his presence.

She glanced over her shoulder and smiled. "It's always better the next day. All those seasonings have had time to blend together and gain a little strength. I hope it's not too spicy for you today."

"Nah. I like spicy." Sinking onto the same barstool he'd sat at the evening before, he watched her. She'd taken off her black blazer and hung it on the back of the chair, clearly exposing her gun...and the way her slacks sat low on her slender hips and hugged her curves.

Realizing he was staring at her ass, Dean rubbed his fingers into his eyelids. Jesus, he needed sleep. Checking out the PI searching for his sister was not the best idea.

Alexa tossed a reheated tortilla from one hand to the other as she brought it to him. "You okay?"

"I didn't sleep much. That's all. I kept trying to figure out how my little sister fell so far."

Sitting next to him, she rested her hand on his forearm.

"My grandmother likes to say every cloud has a silver lining," she said. "With the bad comes the good. Mandy is going through a tough time right now, but had she not fallen so far, you never would have realized she needed help. It's not much comfort, Dean, but this is the beginning of getting her back on track."

"I hope you're right," he said.

"I am." Her confidence didn't exactly lighten his burden, but it sure didn't hurt. "I spoke with your dad this morning."

"And?"

Stirring her stew, she seemed to calculate her words

before speaking. "He says you're too hard on Mandy. Why would he think that?"

"Because he walked out on his kids and has no clue that raising them was a hell of a lot of work." He blew out his breath. "Sorry. That sounded bitter."

She didn't respond. She simply slid a mouthful of posole into her mouth and silently chewed.

"I went to see him last night."

She lifted her brows at him but didn't speak.

"He's so angry at me, and I don't know why. Clearly it has something to do with Mandy, but I can't figure out what. I was never mean to her or hurt her."

"He said something…" She let her words fade as she tried to find the right way to ask about Lily's mental health. "He said the reason he left was because your mother had extreme mood swings, so much so that he began to fear she'd hurt him."

A wry laugh left him. "Mom didn't have mood swings for no reason. She knew he was seeing Trisha, his now-wife. She knew he was a lying, cheating bastard. I could hear them fight sometimes. As for her hurting him… The last big fight they had, she screamed at him that she was going to cut his dick off if he didn't learn to keep it in his pants. I don't think she was crazy, Alexa. I think she was hurt and angry. She never would have hurt him."

"So she was never treated for mental illness?"

"No."

"What was her relationship like with Mandy? Your dad said you and Lily pushed Mandy too hard."

He rolled his tortilla, dipped it in the bowl, and then took a big bite. "Mom and I both butted heads with her quite a bit, especially when she hit her teens."

"Why?"

"Because she could act like a real spoiled brat sometimes. She wanted everything handed to her. Even though our parents were divorced and Dad rarely came around, she knew how to play them against each other. Typical teen stuff, Alexa. She thought she knew everything and was smarter than everybody, but she had a world of growing to do. After Dad left, I took on the role of man of the house. I got a paper route until I was old enough to get a work permit and get a part-time job. Mom needed help, and it was my place to help her, so I stepped up. Mandy thought it was her job to make things harder for everyone, and she knew complaining to Dad would magnify that."

She drew a breath, halted, drew more, and then finally met his gaze. "Dean, I got the distinct impression that he knows where Mandy is. Or at least that he's had some kind of contact with her. He wouldn't confirm that. He just said that she needs a break from the pressure you've put on her and would come home when she was ready."

Anger shot through Dean. "That son of a... He knows how worried I am about her. Why wouldn't he tell me?"

"I don't know. I was hoping you could tell me. Did you and your dad fight about this?"

He pushed his bowl away, his appetite gone, and rested his arms on the counter. "Remember I told you I had to find a drug dealer for Mom? I...I don't know about this shit, Alexa. Buying pot? I hadn't a clue. But I suspected that my stepbrother was a pothead. We're not close or anything, but when I decided to get marijuana for Mom, I asked David for help. He sold me a bag. Dad found out. Even though I explained why, he was pissed that I was enabling David's habits and giving Mandy access to drugs."

Alexa stared at him, processing his confession and what it meant. "So you didn't find some random drug dealer online? You went through your stepbrother."

"Yeah."

"And your dad found out."

"Yeah."

"Is there any chance that the *D* in her journal is *David*?"

Dean considered that. "Um. Maybe. I guess. Could be."

Blatant frustration rolled across her face. She tensed her jaw and huffed out a breath. "If I had known that, I could have taken a different approach when questioning your dad. I deliberately did not bring up Mandy's possible drug use because I assumed he hadn't a clue, and I was trying to respect your request that I not embarrass your sister." She pushed her bowl away too, but she did so angrily. "I cannot help you if you don't tell me everything."

He started to object but held back. "You're right. That was stupid. I apologize."

"I cannot emphasize enough that I am not here to judge you. Whatever you think is too embarrassing to share, believe that I have seen and heard so much worse. This line of work doesn't often allow for me to see the best side of people. You bought drugs for your dying mom. So what? Your little sister got caught up in trouble. Lots do. My job is to find Mandy as quickly as possible. Not point out past mistakes. Understand?"

He nodded. He did understand—not only Alexa's role here but that hiding some long-ago secret was foolish. He'd known that when he didn't tell her the entire truth. But he'd lied about those little things for so long, it hadn't felt like lying anymore. "I got it."

"Good. Is there anything else you'd like to tell me?"

Shifting uncomfortably, he spun his stool to face her and clutched his hands between his knees. "Once, when Mandy was three months old, I went into her room and got her out of her crib. I wasn't supposed to hold her without Mom or Dad, but they never really let me hold her anyway. They said I'd drop her. I wanted to prove that I was big enough to take care of her. They were right. I dropped her. I panicked and put her back in her crib and then hid in the closet so Mom wouldn't know the reason she was crying was because of me."

Alexa dipped her head down and blinked her big brown eyes, but he still saw the little grin she was obviously trying to hide grow. "What does that have to do with her disappearance?"

"I don't know. But for the sake of transparency—"

"Oh"—she playfully shoved his shoulder—"you know what I mean."

She laughed, and the symphonic sound eased the tension in Dean's chest. For some reason he couldn't breathe thinking she was upset with him. He'd spent years mourning his mom and months fearing for his sister. His connections with any other emotions had nearly been severed, but seeing the smile on Alexa's face reminded him there was more than to life than fear and sadness.

He hadn't felt close to anyone for a long time. Not that he was close to Alexa. He'd met her just over twenty-four hours ago, but she supported his concerns. She was on his side. He had needed that more than he'd realized, and the notion that he could lose that because he'd failed to be completely honest spiked a different kind of fear in him. One he didn't fully understand.

She rolled her eyes and shook her head. "Is there anything else I need to know about Mandy, your father, David, you, or anyone else who may have information on her disappearance?"

"I don't think so."

"Any other secrets you're hiding that could help me find your sister?"

He shook his head. "No."

"Your father isn't going to talk to either one of us. Do you think David would talk to you?"

"He might. I don't have much contact with him, even less after the whole pot deal thing blew up. Dad didn't want me to have anything to do with him."

Alexa nodded. "Find time to call your stepbrother and ask him if he knows anything about Mandy. Okay?"

"Okay."

"Good. Now eat. If you don't, I'm going to tell my grandmother, and she'll think you don't like her cooking. It will break her heart."

"I don't want to break your grandmother's heart." He took two big bites before dabbing his chin with a napkin. "You know all about my family. Tell me about yours."

"My grandmother and parents came to America when my mother was pregnant with my older sister. The little town they were from was being overrun with gangs. They didn't want to raise a family there. It was too unstable. Papi opened a little grocery store in the neighborhood where they settled. He worked there until he passed away from a heart attack. Mami sold the store because she didn't think women should run businesses."

"Huh. What does she think about HEARTS? My understanding is the business is owned and operated by a team of women."

The smile that crossed her face was warm and tender. "She knows better now. She's very proud of her girls. And she does consider us all to be *her* girls."

"That's great. And your sister? What does she do?"

That warmth on her lips faded, taking on a sadness he saw in his own reflection these days. "Um, actually, Lanie was abducted a long time ago."

"Oh, Alexa. I'm so sorry. I didn't—"

"You couldn't have known." She put her hand to his arm and squeezed. "I don't share that information with clients openly because..."

The despondency in her eyes told him why. "Because it didn't end well."

"Because I don't know the ending. She was never seen again. No remains were found, no sightings in faraway places. She's just gone, Dean. That's not the kind of thing people want to hear when their loved one is missing."

"No, I guess not." Since she was always so quick to comfort him with a touch, he didn't hesitate in putting his other hand over hers, where it rested on his arm. "I'm sorry."

"I haven't given up. I keep a file in my office. Sometimes I pull it out and go over everything I've learned, hoping that a light bulb will go off. I know that sounds foolish—"

"It doesn't," he interrupted firmly. "It absolutely doesn't. I'll never stop looking for Mandy. If it takes years, I'll never give up hope of finding her and bringing her home. Do you have any leads on your sister?"

"No."

That one little word carried so much hopelessness, he felt the weight of it on his soul. Sliding his arm from under her hand, he draped it over her shoulders and brought her closer to him. "I can't imagine."

"I shouldn't have dumped this on you, Dean."

"You didn't."

"I don't want to add fuel to the fire of your concerns. My sister's disappearance is nothing like Mandy's. Mandy left a trail. We just have to follow it."

Brushing his hand over her hair, he took far too much

notice of how soft the strands felt as he caressed them. When he reached the end of her hair, he ran his fingers over her again. He had to. "I trust you. I know you're doing everything you can. For my sister and your sister."

"I am," she whispered. "I'm going to find Mandy."

"And... What's your sister's name?"

"Lanie."

"You'll find out what happened to Lanie. I believe that."

Tilting her face to his, she smiled, and his breath caught at the jolt her eye contact sent through him. He suspected she felt it as well, because she blinked, sat a bit straighter, and then looked away. She picked up her spoon again and scooped out a big bit of pork. "Eat," she said, not looking at him. "Or I'll tell Abuela on you."

[5]

THERE HAD BEEN so many things Alexa dreaded in the course of being a private investigator, but taking Dean the photos Sam had printed out was definitely in the top five. Make that top three. Dean was trying to be strong, but Alexa had sensed from the day he hired her that it wouldn't take much to make him lose himself in the grief, fear, and self-blame that consumed so many people when their loved ones got mixed up in something sinister.

The images in the envelope were going to tear him apart. Alexa was going to have to fight to keep him focused on finding Mandy and getting her the help she clearly needed instead of allowing himself to sink into the darkness that was bound to fill his mind. Pulling into his driveway, she looked over the little house and considered all he had already been through. The loss of his mom still haunted him. Whenever he spoke of her, his voice softened just a bit, his shoulders stooped a little, and his eyes glazed.

He hadn't been able to save his mom, but he could save his sister. Alexa was going to have to remind him of that repeatedly as they delved into the uglier side of humanity to find her.

Drawing one more breath, she grabbed the envelope and headed for the front door. She pressed the doorbell and then stepped back, giving him time to answer. This time, however, the door opened almost immediately.

He smiled, and nervous energy rolled through her stomach. She didn't take the time to analyze it—obviously she was anxious about the news she was about to share. And when that sensation had hit her the evening prior, it was in response to telling him about Lanie. And when he looked into her eyes and her heart tripped over itself, well, that was because she felt so sorry for what he was going through.

That was all it was.

"I wasn't expecting you."

"Sorry. I should have called."

He stepped aside and let her in. Her gaze was immediately drawn to the trio of wooden pumpkins sitting in the entryway. She followed him into the house, stopping in the entrance to the living room.

"You're decorating?" she asked.

He ran his hand over his hair in that way that seemed to indicate he was nervous or upset. "I couldn't focus on work today. I just... I promised I'd be better at this brother thing when Mandy comes home, but waiting until she gets home seems pointless, doesn't it?" Looking at Alexa, he seemed to be seeking her approval. "I should start working on that now, don't you think?"

"Dean, you're doing everything you can to find her. You're an amazing brother. Don't let this make you doubt that."

"I didn't decorate for Christmas last year."

She didn't quite understand his fixation on that perceived failure, but she was more than aware that stress didn't always present in the most logical way. When Lanie first went missing, her mother was determined to have her favorite meal at the ready upon her return. Mami must have made a thousand tamales. More than they could ever eat. She'd hide in the kitchen for hours rolling masa and shredded pork into dried corn husks.

Walking to a box of decorations, Alexa smiled at the foot-tall Frankenstein's monster she pulled out. He didn't look nearly as frightening as the book portrayed. This guy had lopsided eyes and a big smile painted across his face. The friendliest monster Alexa had ever seen.

"Mandy used to scare easily," Dean explained. "Mom made sure Halloween was silly around here."

"Not everyone enjoys being spooked." She set the decoration back into the box.

Holding up two bags of Easter eggs, he twisted his mouth. "I don't know what I'm supposed to do with these. Mom bought them. Maybe she just tucked them in the wrong box."

"She was probably going to use those to hand out candy." She smiled at the confusion on his face. "You put candy inside and draw faces on them. Like pumpkins on the orange ones or witches on the green. It's just a different way for the kids to choose what they want instead of picking based on the candy inside."

He looked at the bags. "Huh. Seems like a lot of trouble to give away a chocolate bar."

"Sometimes the anticipation is half the fun."

Tossing the eggs back into the box, he let out a long, dramatic breath. "I don't know what the hell I'm doing. I thought this would distract me."

Setting the envelope on the table next to the box, Alexa grabbed the eggs. "Bring me a marker."

She had the bag opened when he offered her a black permanent marker. She didn't have the best drawing abilities, but by the time she finished marking the blue egg in her hand, the face distinctly belonged to a vampire. She turned it to him, smiling. "See? Kids get a kick out of this stuff." Selecting a green egg, she drew a face like the Frankenstein's monster decoration. "Then you put little candies inside. When the kids come for trick-or-treat, you'll have a bowlful of fun little treats. You'll be the most popular house on the block."

He snorted. "Fat chance. The Kingmans two houses over give away full-size Snickers every year."

She frowned and let her shoulders stoop. "Those inconsiderate jerks."

"Yup. Every kid for miles around knows to hit that place up."

"We could break in and replace their stash with little tubes of toothpaste. That would ruin their Halloween cred real quick."

He chuckled. "That's not a bad idea."

She liked his smile so much more than his sulking. Not that he didn't have plenty to sulk about. Which reminded her that she was there to add to the list. She couldn't bring herself to do ruin this moment. She wasn't ready to add more stress to his already long list. Glancing at her watch, she confirmed she had a few hours before Jack wanted everyone at the office. Ignoring her reason for showing up at Dean's house, she reached into the box of decorations. "Did your mom have a certain place she put things every year, or did she change it up?"

"She just put things wherever she put them."

"That makes it easier." Holding up a wall hanging, she read over the poem and smiled at the raven painted in the corner. "Front door?"

He hesitated before nodding and taking the sign. As he returned, she was lining three burlap pumpkins on his mantle. He helped her string skeleton lights over his front window and then climbed on a short ladder to pin several bats to the ceiling in the entryway. She stood back, not wanting to get stepped on when he hopped down. The fact that the added height put his denim-clad bottom right in her face wasn't lost on her. Rather than check out his backside, Alexa turned her attention to setting several wooden statues around the fireplace.

When they finished, his home was spectacularly decked out for the holiday. Folding the ladder, he set it aside and joined her in the middle of the room to look around. His little laugh sounded of amazement.

"Mom would approve," he announced.

The warmth in his tone reached Alexa's heart. "Good. I'm glad."

"Mandy would too, I think."

"Well, it is my goal to bring her home in time to get that approval."

"Good goal," he said.

"Have you talked to David?" she asked.

Dean shook his head. "I left him a message. He hasn't called me back. That's not unusual. We aren't exactly close."

"I'm sorry."

"Don't be," he said. "I'm not worried about it. Do you want coffee?"

"Sure."

As he carried the ladder back to the kitchen, Alexa sealed the now-empty box and frowned at the envelope she'd left on the table. She couldn't avoid it forever. At some point, she had to shatter this poor man's heart. Taking the photos, she followed him into the kitchen.

He glanced over his shoulder and then returned his focus to pulling the top off the canister of coffee grounds.

"I'm guessing you didn't pop in to help me decorate. What's up?"

Taking what had somehow become her seat at the counter, she bit her lip and focused on the envelope in her hand. "Sometimes when people get caught up in drugs, they inadvertently get caught up in other things, too. Whether it's because their judgment gets flawed or their addictions get the better of them and they can't find a better way. Sometimes they make choices that we can't fully understand. And sometimes they get pulled into things without realizing or...maybe they get in with the wrong person who takes advantage, or—"

"Alexa?"

She hadn't realized he'd stopped messing with the coffee and had crossed the kitchen to stand on the other side of the counter from her. When she looked up at him, her stomach tightened with dread.

"Did you find Mandy?" he pressed.

"No, but..."

"But what?"

"I asked one of my teammates to search for images of her online. On certain types of sites. Sites where women sometimes..."

Impatience and irritation flickered across his face. "What?"

"It isn't uncommon for drug addicts to..."

"For fuck's sake," he snapped. "Spit it out."

She held his gaze. "Dean, I need you to look at some photos of a prostitute and confirm if it's your sister."

His gaze lowered to the envelope she held out to him and then looked back to her. She thought she could actually see his spirits sink.

"I'm sorry," she whispered.

Snagging the envelope, he ripped it open and reached inside. He didn't pull the pictures out, though. He closed his eyes tight, took three big, deep breaths, and then looked at Alexa. "Do you think it's her?"

Swallowing the knot building in her throat, she nodded. "Yes. I do."

He slid the pictures out, and the choked sound that left his throat was all the answer she needed. The underweight girl in the picture wearing just enough clothing to cover her most intimate parts was his sister. Her short dark hair was unkempt. Some men might even find her stoned, messy appearance sexy, but Dean looked like he was going to be sick.

Alexa didn't have to ask why. She'd memorized the photo Sam had found in her search of the Dark Web. Mandy's pimp had several girls who looked just like her. Too thin, eyes glazed, doing their best to look alluring for the camera to tempt someone into paying them for sex. Money they would then give to the man in charge of everything, from what and when they ate to when and where they had sex for money in exchange for supplying them with their drug of choice.

Pushing the pictures aside, without even looking at the other images, he turned his back to Alexa. "Where is she?" he asked, his voice barely audible.

"This listing was in Chicago, but..."

Facing her, he questioned her with his eyes.

She tried to swallow, but her mouth was dry. "I'm trying to find... Depending on..."

"Alexa. Jesus, just tell me."

"Pimps tend to sell and trade their girls frequently to shake things up for their clientele. These pictures were taken two weeks ago. Now that you've confirmed it's Mandy, I'm going to reach out to a human trafficking unit in the area and ask for their assistance in locating her."

"Human...trafficking?"

"She isn't doing this to herself, Dean. She's being sold. And from her appearance, the weight loss and dilated pupils, she's either being forced into it for drugs or she's being kept so stoned she doesn't fully comprehend what is happening to her."

"Someone out there is...selling my sister?"

"I'm sorry," she whispered again.

Dean turned his back to Alexa again. She sat silently, waiting for the inevitable wrecking ball of emotion to hit him. She wasn't sure what form that would take—crying, screaming, raw rage—but she didn't doubt it was coming. He'd just seen photographic evidence that his little sister was a drugged-out prostitute. Most likely because of the man who had listed her on a website like she was a piece of furniture for sale instead of a living, breathing nineteen-year-old girl.

"What the fucking hell?" he screamed. Raking his fingers through his hair, he heaved a few breaths before crossing the kitchen. Swiping his arm across the counter, he cleared it of the coffee pot and canister of grounds. Both crashed to the floor with a deafening collision. Glass and plastic shattered. He dug his fingers into his hair and turned to face Alexa. The soul-crushing pain in his eyes broke her heart. "Don't say it," he warned. "Don't you dare tell me how fucking sorry you are."

She didn't take his anger personally. His rage wasn't directed at her. She knew that, but he must not have realized.

He dropped his hands and exhaled. "I didn't mean—"

"I know," she stated. "This isn't what you had hoped to learn. But we are one step closer to finding her, Dean."

He rested one hand on his hip and pressed the other to his mouth. After several long seconds, he blew out his breath. "Could you leave? Please."

She opened her mouth. The last thing she wanted was for him to process this alone.

"Please. Alexa. I need you to go. Take those fucking pictures with you."

Grabbing the envelope, she stood and tried to gauge him. She didn't want to leave him, but she had no right to stay when he didn't want her to. "You have my cell number. Call me if you need me."

She paused, hoping he'd change his mind, but he didn't. She left him standing there. Closing the front door behind her, she read the sign and muttered, "Double, double, toil and trouble, indeed."

The drive back to the HEARTS office didn't ease her

stress much. When she walked in, she frowned at Sam. "Dean confirmed the girl's identity. You found her."

"Oh no. How'd he take it?"

"About how any brother would take finding out his sister is being sold on the open market." Glancing at her watch, she checked the time. "Everyone's here?" she whispered.

Sam smiled and rubbed her hands together. "Jack is on his way."

Okay. That lifted Alexa's spirits. Walking into her office, she put the printed photos of Mandy into a file and dropped behind her desk. She'd been nearly one hundred percent certain of the identity of the woman in the photo, so she'd already located the number of an official in Chicago. She made the call and then sat back and waited for an answer so she could get the ball rolling on pinning down which sleazeball of a pimp was selling Dean's sister.

DEAN DIDN'T KNOW HOW HE WAS SUPPOSED TO respond to Alexa's news. He did know he hadn't responded in the most effective way. He should have set his emotions aside and pushed Alexa for more information and her plan to locate the asshole taking advantage of his baby sister. Breaking his coffee pot and dumping a near-full container of grounds hadn't been a bit productive. Lashing out at Alexa had been even less so. She was doing her job, and she was damn good at it. She'd been working this case for just over forty-eight hours and had already come closer to Mandy than he'd been in months.

Of course, he hadn't been looking in the gutter for his sister. How the hell had she gotten caught up in this? He couldn't understand it. Her life hadn't been so bad. Yeah, Mom had expectations of her, but she'd never treated Mandy badly. She had never neglected her or abused her. How did she... How could she...

Human trafficking?

He sat at his desk researching the topic, and his stomach turned more and more sour with every website, every news story, every horrific detail he learned. His mind was going a million miles an hour trying to figure out how this had happened to his sister. He still couldn't make sense of it. This still didn't seem possible. Maybe that hadn't been Mandy after all. Maybe he'd seen her in the image because he was so desperate to find her.

He needed to look at the picture again. He needed to look more closely. He needed to step back from the emotion of it all and really look at that girl. Maybe...maybe she wasn't Mandy.

Are you at your office? he texted Alexa.

Yes. Are you okay?

Is it okay if I swing by?

Of course, she immediately responded.

He drove on autopilot, his mind still rolling over any excuse he could think of to justify why that wasn't Mandy in the photo and why she couldn't possibly be selling her body. He'd damn near convinced himself by the time he pulled into the parking lot of the HEARTS office. He stared at the brick building, working up the nerve to go in.

Not because he was nervous about seeing Alexa, but because deep inside, he knew the moment he told her of his convictions, she'd give him that sympathetic smile as her eyes softened. Then she'd put her hand on his arm and rip the rug right out from under him. She'd tell him the truth he already knew—Mandy had turned to prostitution —and his world would crash around him yet again.

He was so damned tired of his world crashing around him. He couldn't remember the last time things had been right, even for a moment. The sound of a car door jolted him from his miserable thoughts.

A man standing at the car next to him was trying to balance three covered dishes, a long box, and several bags. He was clearly struggling with his load. Shoving his car door open, Dean jumped out. "Need some help?"

The man grinned. "I need four extra hands."

Dean took the precarious packages off the top and focused on the top window of the bakery box. Through the clear plastic, the words *Congratulations, Holly and Jack* were written in neat script. "Looks like a party is about to start."

The man's eyes widened. "Wait. Who are you?"

"Dean Campbell. Alexa is helping me find my sister."

The stranger offered one of those supportive smiles. "Oh, I'm sorry."

"And you are?" Dean pressed.

"Josh Simmons. Eva's better half. Don't tell her I said that."

Dean laughed softly. "My lips are sealed."

Josh shifted the dishes in his hands. "Also, you didn't see this cake. Holly doesn't know Jack is going to propose. Actually, nobody does. Except Eva and me. Sam asked us to get the cake. Well, then we had to tell Jack's mom because she works in a bakery and Eva thought she might be offended if we got a cake from somewhere else. I'm rambling."

"A little," Dean said.

"I'm nervous. For Jack. I mean... I think Holly will say yes. Eva thinks Holly will say yes. But she might not, and then things will be awkward."

Dean nodded. "Probably."

"Do you think you could get the door? This stuff is getting a little heavy." At the front door, Josh stopped and looked at Dean. "Okay, so you don't know anything about this. This conversation never happened."

"I didn't hear a thing. Oh." He tilted his head toward the box. "You might want to cover that cake, though."

Josh looked down at the red lettering staring up at him. "Shit."

Chuckling, Dean put the bags back on top of the cake box and then took it from Josh, who still held the casserole dishes. With one hand securely balancing the cake box, Dean opened the door and let Josh go ahead of him. He greeted Sam as he followed Josh into the conference room.

A stack of plates and silverware had been piled in the middle.

"Won't she be suspicious of all this?" he whispered.

Josh eased the dishes down. "Nope. We always have dinner on Fridays." He put the bags on the table as he looked around. "I gotta hide that cake." Eyeing a chair in the corner, he took the box from Dean, set it on the seat, and then covered it with his coat. "What do you think?"

"Nobody will notice unless they're looking."

Josh scowled. "They're PIs. They're always looking." Turning the chair so the back was to the room, he tucked his jacket around it. "Now?"

"That's good. Really."

"Awesome." Hands on his hips, Josh faced Dean. "I'm sorry about your sister. Alexa is great at what she does. You're in good hands." His cheeks blushed. "I don't mean *you*. I mean...your case."

Dean grinned. "I gathered what you meant." Though the thought of having Alexa's hands on him wasn't at all off-putting. In fact he'd come to enjoy her reassuring touches. However, he didn't think he was so transparent that Josh should have picked up on it.

Josh winced. "I know you did." Exhaling, he shrugged. "I'm nervous. I ramble when I'm nervous."

"Right. Well, I hope things go well. I'm going to try to steal a few minutes with Alexa so you guys can get on with your dinner." He left Josh looking as anxious as if he were the one about to propose. He was nearing the reception desk when Sam hopped up.

"She's expecting you," she said. She led him down a hallway past several open doors and then finally stopped and gestured for him to enter one.

Alexa was on the phone but waved him in. She offered Dean that kindly smile he was expecting. "Thank you so much, Detective Wilson. I really appreciate your assistance. I'll wait to hear from you." She ended the call and rounded her desk. "How are you?"

"Embarrassed. I'm sorry I responded like that."

"Don't be." As he'd already come to anticipate, she put her hand to his arm, and her touch soothed him as much as her smile. "I completely understand."

"I started thinking. Maybe that isn't her, Alexa. Maybe the girl in the photo just looks close enough that I mistook her for Mandy. I need to see it again."

She opened her mouth as if she were going to argue but seemed to think better of it. She leaned over her desk, opened a file, and snatched the little white envelope. She held it out to him, but he hesitated in taking it. When he did, he held his breath as he lifted the flap. The pictures slid out effortlessly, and he forced himself to examine the photos, to really look at them.

Swallowing the lump in his throat, he stared into the eyes of the girl. They were glazed. And hollow. Her cheeks were sunken in enough to make out her cheekbones. The makeup she wore was so much heavier than he remembered his sister ever wearing. Her hair, which Mandy always kept brushed, seemed shaggy and unwashed.

Blinking, forcing himself to look lower, he took in the way her ribs were visible. Not like she was on the verge of starving, but she was clearly not eating well or often. The first time he'd looked at the pictures, he hadn't looked behind the first one. He forced himself to do so now. The second photo was a screenshot of her statistics.

Five-foot-three. Just like Mandy.

Brown eyes, brown hair. Just like Mandy.

Nineteen. Just like Mandy.

Dean creased his brown and looked at Alexa. "What does Certified Clean mean?"

She inhaled, exhaled, and then whispered, "Her pimp is guaranteeing she has no STDs. Some men prefer... He can charge more if men don't have to use protection."

Her words were like a knife cutting out Dean's heart. Anger ran through him like a speeding train, and he filled with a rage he'd never known before. "How can men look at this girl and think it's okay to buy her like... What kind of man would see her like this and not care that she's in trouble?"

"Unfortunately, Dean, there are a lot of men who would see her and only see an opportunity to take advantage of her."

Dropping into the chair in front of her desk, he put the pictures back and tossed the envelope onto Alexa's desk. "That's her. That's definitely Mandy." Leaning forward, he slid his fingers into his hair and planted his elbows on his knees. Closing his eyes, he did his best to fight the tears that were pressing against the back of his eyes. Never in a million fucking years would he have thought he'd be sitting in a private investigator's office being told that his baby sister was a certified clean prostitute. "What the fuck?" he said under his breath and sniffed back his emotions.

He didn't see Alexa come to his side. He sensed her. He felt her heat before she put her arm around his back. He smelled the subtle but distinct musk that surrounded her before she leaned in and held him. And he fell into her comfort before he could stop himself. Wrapping his arms around her waist, he pulled her close, pressing his cheek to her chest as she hugged him.

Nothing made sense to him. Not Mandy throwing her life away. Or her turning to drugs and prostitution. And definitely not the solace he found in Alexa. He didn't even know her, but just feeling her arms around him brought a wave of assuagement to his soul. When she was close to him, offering her little pets and smiles, he believed that everything would be okay, that somehow Mandy could survive this. He had hope when Alexa was this close to him. He clung to that feeling, to her, until someone rapped on the door and opened it.

"Oh! I...uh...I-I'm sorry," a woman stuttered. Her umber skin shaded with red at her obvious embarrassment. Tucking wayward black curls behind her ear, she gestured vaguely toward the hallway. "I just wanted to let you know we're serving dinner."

"It's okay, Tika," Alexa said just over a whisper as Dean broke his tight hold on her hips. "I'll be there soon."

Dean ran his hand over his hair as the door clicked closed. "Sorry."

"Don't be." Alexa ran her hand over his hair as well, but her touch was far more tender than his had been. Her touch was like a balm on his blistered soul. Cupping his face, she tenderly lifted his chin. "I know this is so much to take in. Don't apologize for how tough this is. I'm here for you, Dean. I want to help you through this."

"You're a PI, not a counselor."

"I can be both."

Exhaling, he swallowed. "I should go. Your dinner—"

"Will keep."

Recalling how nervous Josh had been about the impending proposal, Dean shook his head. "You don't want to keep your friends waiting. I'm good."

"I doubt that. Do you want to go for a drink or—"

"No. Alexa, you need to be here. For dinner."

She lowered her gaze. "Usually I would disagree, but tonight is kind of special."

"You know about..." he said.

Her eyes bulged. "*You* know about...?"

Surprisingly, a little smile touched his lips. "I met Josh on my way in. He needed help carrying everything. I saw the cake."

"Ah," Alexa said. "Well. Yes, I should be here for that. Why don't you join us?"

"I'm not going to crash your friend's marriage proposal, Alexa."

She shrugged. "The more the merrier."

"I'm afraid I'm not much in the mood for what's to come."

She lowered her face and nodded. "I get that, but I'm worried about you."

"I'm not going to do something stupid, if that's what you're thinking."

"I'm not," she was quick to say. "But that doesn't mean you should be alone right now. I have no idea what we're having for dinner, but I'd like to bring you leftovers. If you don't mind me stopping by to check on you later."

"I don't mind," he said quietly. "In fact, I'd like that very much."

6

ALEXA DID her best to focus on the chattering around her. She usually loved team dinners. Tonight's should have been especially exciting, but she couldn't stop replaying the absolutely broken look in Dean's eyes as he finally accepted what had become of his sister. She couldn't imagine what he was thinking or feeling.

She barely touched the ham and potato casserole Josh had scooped onto her plate, and she had no desire to share in the cake they were going to cut into. She just wanted to pack up dinner for Dean and go check on him.

Tika nudged her. "What was that about?"

"He just found out his sister has been pulled into a human trafficking ring."

Tika winced, the smooth, dark skin of her forehead creasing as she squeezed her eyes shut. "God. I'm sorry."

"She's nineteen, Tik. And if the photos are any indication, she's so strung out, she doesn't have a clue what's happening to her."

"That's a blessing in its own way. Better for her mind to be a fog than to realize she's being sold for sex."

Alexa nodded her agreement. "I'll get her out, and he'll get her the help she needs. She'll get past this."

"I'm sure she'll get through it," Tika said. "He's cute."

Alexa started at the sudden change of subject. "What?"

Tika smiled. "The man who was wrapped in your arms. He's cute."

Rolling her eyes, she chuckled. "And distraught. Don't read into it."

"If you say so." Tika nudged her again and returned her attention to the conversation around them. One by one, the women updated their teammates on their cases. Even Josh and Jack took turns talking about their week during Friday night dinners, even though they weren't technically part of the team.

When it was Jack's turn tonight, however, his cheeks turned red and his mother nearly burst at his side. She muttered something in her native Egyptian tongue that caused Holly to jolt, and Jack to cut his gaze toward his mother with accusation. Alexa didn't understand what was said, but Holly, who had spent quite a bit of her Army tour in the Middle East, clearly had.

"What..." Holly started.

"Hush, woman," Jack said in the firm but teasing tone he used so often with Holly.

Alexa didn't think there could ever be two people better suited for each other. Holly was tough as nails. So was Jack. But they had such a deep tenderness for each other, anyone could see they were meant to be. They had fallen head over heels so quickly it was almost enough to make Alexa believe in soulmates.

They'd met when Holly was working a different missing persons case. Jack, a detective with one of the area departments, was working a similar case. They had joined forces, and that was that. They were bonded forever in a way that had filled the rest of the HEARTS with hope that maybe there really were men out there who could handle pairing with strong women.

Most of them had learned the hard way that relation-ships were a tough thing to get through when the female half was as strong as, or stronger than, the male half. Seeing Jack smile at Holly with so much love and affection definitely gave Alexa some sense she could find that some-day, too.

"What my mother means," Jack said pointedly, "is... Holly, we've been through a lot in our short time together. We've seen some really great times and some dark times. You've seen me at my best and my worst. And vice versa."

Holly's eyes seemed to widen farther with every word he said. She didn't lose her stone-faced facade often, but seeing the surprise clearly written on her face was enough to make Alexa chuckle. Holly slowly opened her mouth as Jack pushed his chair back and got on one knee beside her. The room filled with gasps and dreamy sighs.

"Marry me," Jack said. Not a question or an order, simply an insecure-sounding request as he held out a ring.

"Are you...serious?" Holly asked.

"Only if you plan to say yes," Jack deadpanned. "If you're going to say no, this was a big prank."

"Jack..."

Alexa's heart rolled over and dropped. If Holly said no, Alexa was going to put her in a headlock and drag her down the aisle. Jack was perfect. Absolutely fucking perfect. No man would ever love Holly like he did, and Alexa would not allow her friend to blow this relationship out of the water.

But then Holly's shock broke into a brilliant smile. "Of course I'll marry you, you idiot."

The room filled with happy sighs as Jack slid the engagement ring on Holly's finger. Najwa looked to the heavens and clasped her hands, saying a little prayer, as the HEARTS all jumped up.

Hugs and kisses and *oohs* and *aahs* filled the conference room as Josh unveiled the cake.

"You guys knew?" Holly said accusingly.

Alexa was going to deny, deny, deny, but as she looked around the room, it was obvious that Holly was the only one who hadn't heard about Jack's plan. He gawked at Sam, who simply shrugged.

"Holly didn't know," Sam justified.

"You told Sam and thought it'd be a secret?" Holly asked.

"I needed her help to make sure everyone was here."

He slid his arm around Holly's waist and pulled her closer. "I knew you'd want them here."

Holly put her hand to his cheek, and the newly placed diamond sparkled as she kissed him. Alexa was so happy for her friend she could cry. But she also felt that emptiness in her heart expand ever so slightly.

"Don't cut that yet," Sam ordered. She pulled the office camera out and started snapping photos of the cake and then of Jack and Holly, the ring, the happy couple cutting into the cake, as if it were their wedding instead of their engagement. Happiness filled the room, surrounding them all in some well-deserved exhilaration, but half of Alexa's mind was elsewhere.

As she shared in this joyous occasion, Dean was home thinking of how his sister was being treated like property. Alexa just wanted to grab some food and rush to his side to help him through what was certainly one of the most difficult things he'd ever faced. She walked around the table to where Josh and Eva stood—who were also rubbing it in Alexa's face that she didn't have a significant other to get through life with—and broke up their little hug.

"Josh, do you mind if I borrow one of your dishes? I'd like to take dinner to my client. He's had a rough day."

"Sure thing."

"What about you? You've seemed distracted. Are you okay?" Eva asked, unwrapping herself from Josh's hold.

Alexa frowned. "I just hated telling him about his sister." She didn't have to elaborate. They'd all heard her update as they'd eaten dinner. "He's home alone dwelling on it. I want to check on him."

"Take whatever you need," Josh said.

She did. She took half a casserole and added two large pieces of cake to a plate. Setting those aside, she made her way to Holly and wrapped her in her arms. Holly was not a hugger but seemed to be tolerating her teammates' affections this evening. "Congratulations," Alexa said in her ear.

Leaning back, Holly smiled a rare but beautiful smile. "Thank you. You're going to see Dean?"

"Yeah."

Holly's happy smile softened. "How are you holding up?"

"Better than he is."

"This is a tough situation," Holly said.

"I just want to check on him."

"I understand."

Smiling, Alexa hugged Holly again. "I'm so happy for you." She embraced Jack and told him the same and then left her team to celebrate. She didn't know why she felt such a damn sense of urgency to get to Dean, but she knew he was torturing himself over what was happening to Mandy. Alexa couldn't ease his anguish, but she could make sure he didn't go through it alone. That seemed far more consequential to her at the moment.

She drove as quickly as she could to Dean's and rang the bell. He didn't keep her waiting this time, either. He opened the door and let her in almost instantly.

Alexa held up the casserole. "Hungry?"

"Yeah." As they walked into the kitchen, he looked at the counter where they'd shared their last two meals together. "Mind if we sit at the table? I need to break the bad habit of eating in the kitchen. Mom let that go for breakfast and lunch, but she said dinner was family time that should be spent at the table. Not that I have any family to eat with right now."

The sadness in his voice made her heart ache for him. She'd lost her sister and her father, but she was so close to her mother and grandmother. She never had to eat alone. Sometimes, even when she wanted to, she couldn't. Sitting at his table to share a meal while trying to support him through his troubles appealed to her more than she thought made sense. "That'd be great."

He gathered plates and silverware and led her to the dining room. She filled his plate before sitting next to him, draping a napkin across her lap.

"I don't want to talk about it," he said. "I know we have to. I have a million questions. But I can't talk about it right now. If I keep thinking about this, I'm going to lose my mind."

"Okay."

He stabbed at the potatoes on his plate but didn't lift the fork to his mouth. "So. Holly said yes?"

She smiled. "She did."

"I'm glad to hear some good news. How many of you are married?"

"None of us, actually. Holly and Eva are the only ones even in a relationship."

He looked at her. "Oh?"

Alexa shrugged. It was her turn to focus on her meal more intently than necessary. "This job is demanding. If we're on a case, the hours can be brutal. I once sat in my car for thirteen hours during a stakeout. Most men wouldn't necessarily understand that I have to miss dinner or cancel plans because I'm too busy staring at someone's back door to make sure they aren't breaking the law in some way. It just..." She shrugged. "It takes a special kind of man to understand what we do."

"But Jack understands?"

Alexa told him how Holly and Jack had worked a case together. How they'd saved each other. How they'd become inseparable. How they'd fallen so deeply in love, she couldn't imagine them ever falling out.

"Why do you look so sad?" Dean asked, drawing Alexa from her story.

"What?"

"You're sitting here telling me how one of your closest friends is so happy, and you look so...melancholy."

"Do I?"

He nodded. "You do. Why?"

She pushed her plate away. Over the course of her tale, she'd taken bite after bite until her dinner was gone. "Cake?"

"Answers," he countered.

Laughing lightly, she sat back. "Sometimes... Okay, all

the time, I wish I had that. I love my family and my friends, but I don't have the best luck with men."

"Why?"

She stared at him for a long time. "Because I give too much. I care too much. I feel too much." Frowning, she served herself a slice of the cake. She needed the sweet treat even if he wasn't interested. "I have this way of diving in headfirst and falling hard. And then realizing I'm the only one falling. I'm one of those bleeding-heart types, you know? I think losing my father and my sister when I was so young taught me how important it is to let people know how I feel about them. That's not always a good thing. I fall too easily. That scares men off more than it endears them."

Dean's gaze turned intense. "Not everyone appreciates what they have when they have it. It took Mom getting sick for me to realize I needed to be a better son. And Mandy disappearing before realizing I should have been a more attentive brother. It's a good thing that you see the value in people without having to lose them first."

She chuckled. "Tell that to the rest of your half of the species. Women like me scare them."

"Women like you?"

"I want the whole package. The hand holding and secret looks and sneaking kisses. I want romance and wooing and a man who isn't afraid to give me that. It's too much. I know it's too much, but I don't feel right pretending that I don't want those things."

"You shouldn't pretend. If that's what you want, then that's what you should get."

She frowned. "But the odds of finding that aren't so great. My bar is too high. I'm setting every poor man I date up for failure."

Dean put his hand on hers. "No. You're telling him what to aim for. To hell with any man who can't reach it."

"I only have this one life," she said quietly. "I don't want to live it with someone who doesn't cherish every moment I give him. Does that make sense?"

"Yes," he stated firmly.

Heaving a sigh, she stared at her cake. "Holly and Jack have that. I know it's out there. I just have to find it."

Glancing up, expecting to see some kind of smirk or disbelief on Dean's face, Alexa jolted. He wasn't looking at her like she was a foolish woman with her head in the clouds. He was looking at her like he could read her mind, see her innermost thoughts, and was debating whether he liked what he saw.

"I said too much," she stuttered out.

Silence lingered between them before he reached for his slice of cake. He put it on his plate and dug in before dropping his fork. "I'm going to Chicago," he said.

She wasn't surprised. She'd expected to hear that from him. "Not until I hear back from the detective I spoke with. If he confirms she's still in the area, we'll go together."

Dean smiled slightly, nodded his approval, and then finished his cake.

ROLLING ONTO HIS SIDE, DEAN STARED INTO THE darkness. His brain was bouncing all over the place, remembering everything from the photos of Mandy to the wistful look on Alexa's face as she spoke about what she wanted in a relationship.

She seemed to think she'd never find that. He thought it was crazy that she hadn't already. Not only was she beautiful and thoughtful and brilliant, but she was sexy as hell. The way she stared him down, as if picking his brain apart, kept him enthralled. Her tenderness kept him sane. He thought he'd be lucky to have a woman like that in his life.

A quick glance at the clock convinced him that his attempt at sleeping was futile. His options were to get up and do something to distract himself or lie there obsessing about his missing sister and the woman looking for her. Either situation was going to make him crazy.

Kicking the blankets off, he flipped on the bedside light and headed straight for the closet. He tossed a small duffel bag on the bed and dug out three pairs of jeans, a handful of socks and boxer briefs, and several T-shirts and stuffed them inside. Even if Mandy wasn't in Chicago any longer, someone there had seen her and might be able to tell him where to look next. He'd head out in the morning, with or without Alexa.

He was zipping the bag before logic kicked in that without Alexa, he'd never even get close to finding his sister. Alexa had called the detective in charge of the human trafficking department. He was looking into Mandy's case. He was going to let her know if she should come to Chicago. If there was no sign of Mandy in the area, there was no point in going. Alexa had told him this. More than once. And he had listened. He had heard. But he had nothing else to go on, and he had spent too long sitting still, twiddling his thumbs, and hoping for the best. He'd done all the being "patient" he could handle.

When she'd first disappeared, his dad had said be patient. Then the police had said be patient. Now he had to be patient while Alexa waited to hear from the detective. Damn it. He was out of patience. Especially now that he knew what kind of trouble his sister had landed herself in.

Jesus. Prostitution? Drugs? How had he not seen her going down this road? Sure, she was away at college and he only saw her every other month or so, but he tried to stay in touch. He tried to keep up with her on social media and over the phone. How had he missed that she was in so much trouble? And why hadn't she told him?

Maybe his dad was right. Maybe Dean had been too hard on her. He just wanted what was best for her. He wanted to push her to be the best possible version of herself that she could be. Had he pushed too hard?

He didn't think he had. He hadn't tried to. Thinking back, he didn't think his mother had either. In fact, he'd once told her that she coddled Mandy too much. That she was being too easy on her and giving her too much. His mother hadn't had a lot of money; she was a single parent struggling to make ends meet. But she'd bent over backward to make sure Mandy could participate in any activity she showed interest in. She worked overtime hours to pay fees and keep Mandy in name-brand clothing.

Things Dean had never had. He'd worked part time to help pay his fees, and all he'd played was basketball. He never had top-of-the-line clothing. Maybe he resented that more than he'd realized. The first big fight he and Mandy had after their mother passed away was Dean's refusal to buy her new jeans when she had perfectly good ones in her drawer. She insisted that colored jeans were the new trend and she needed *just one pair*. He told her to get a job and buy them.

That had gone over about as well as telling her that he'd take her to a consignment shop to buy her prom dress. She was only going to wear the thing one night. He wasn't paying hundreds of dollars for something new.

Their mom had spoiled her, and when Dean didn't continue that trend, he was the bad guy. And their father had reinforced her thoughts on that. He had given her money for jeans and a prom dress. Dean had rolled his eyes and told her she'd never learn the value of anything if it was always given to her. Maybe that was too much to expect from a teenager who had just lost her mother.

Raking his fingers through his hair, he dropped onto the bed as another thread of guilt weaved through his brain. He should have protected her. Spoiled or not, she needed him to protect her. He should have known she was in trouble. Somehow. He should have known.

The phone on his nightstand chirped, indicating he had a new text. The clock next to the phone reminded him it was two in the morning. Jumping up, he snatched his cell, disconnecting the cord so it didn't snag. The text was from an unknown number.

Dean? U there?

Mandy?

I need u.

His heart pounded and fingers trembled as he typed, *I know. Where r u? R u ok?*

Idk. I'm sorry.

Call me.

I cant.

Damn it. He wanted to scream. *R u in danger?*

Come get me.

Where? He waited. And waited. *Mandy?* She didn't respond. *Mandy? Plz. I'm trying to find u.*

Silence. He pressed the button to call the phone and closed his eyes as the ringing on the line went unanswered until a robotic voice told him the voicemail for that number had not been set up.

Mandy? he texted.

Clutching the phone, he stood and paced as panic settled in his bones. Finally he texted, *I'll find u. I promise. I love you. No matter what.*

Then he scrolled through his numbers. "She texted me," he said as soon as Alexa's groggy voice answered.

"Mandy was texting me. But then she stopped. I think she's in trouble. I mean immediate trouble."

Alexa cleared her throat. "Can you screenshot it and text it to me?"

Pulling the phone from his ear, he sent her several screenshots. "Did you get them?"

"One sec."

"I'm sorry," he said as she yawned out the words. "I know it's late, but I thought—"

"You did the right thing calling me," she said. "Hang on."

He started pacing again, waiting for her response.

"I got the images," she said. "Let me call you back in a few minutes. I need to boot up my laptop and try to trace this number."

"Alexa, she sounds scared. Don't you think?"

Alexa was quiet for a moment before saying, "She seemed distressed. That doesn't mean she's in immediate danger. Maybe she just wants to come home and isn't sure how to do that. Let me trace this number. I'll call you back in a few minutes."

She ended the call, but she might as well have cut his last remaining tie to reality. Mandy was in danger. Immediate danger. He felt it. She was reaching out to him to save her, and he was helpless. Desperate, he did the only thing he could think of. He called his dad.

He didn't answer the call. Not that Dean was surprised. He did, however, leave a message at the beep. "Mandy is in trouble. If you know where she is, you need to tell me so I can find her." There was raw anger in his tone, and he hadn't done a damn thing to hide it.

Isolated. That was the only way he could describe what he was feeling in that moment. Isolated from anyone who cared about him or his sister. Terrified. That was another good word. He'd lost Mandy to this world, but he couldn't face that he might not be able to save her from it. She had gotten in over her head somehow, but she wanted out. Her text messages proved that in his mind. She wanted out. He just had to find her.

He startled when the phone in his hand rang. Alexa. "Well?"

"That call came from Chicago. Pack a bag. We'll leave in the morning."

"I've already packed my bag. We'll leave now."

"Dean—"

"It's about five and a half hours, Alexa. We'll get there first thing in the morning."

"We'll get there exhausted and unable to think."

He was silent for a moment. "Do you really think I'll sleep now? Will you?"

She was quiet before heaving a loud sigh in his hear. "Stay put. I'll pick you up in half an hour."

7

THE DRIVE to Chicago was unpleasant, to say the least. Alexa did her best to keep Dean calm, but he was restless and impatient. They stopped for gas just outside the city, and she was tempted to tell him to put the coffee pot down as he filled a big disposable cup, but she didn't.

His behavior was to be expected. She'd be more concerned if he weren't so irritable. Calm and cool were not the responses she'd expect given the events that had unfolded overnight. As she parked at the police station, she sank back in the driver's seat and looked over at him. "I don't know what's going to happen in there, Dean."

"I know."

"It might be best if you let me go in and talk to them. You can find us a hotel and crash. Just text me where you are—"

"I need to be there." Rolling his head to her, he let out

a long breath. "I've done enough research that I know what's happening to her. It will be difficult to hear, but...I can't waste any more time being oversensitive. The faster we find her, the faster we get her into recovery. Let's just get in there and find my sister."

"Okay. If it gets to be too much, you can leave. I'll let you know everything."

"I'm not leaving." He opened the car door and stepped out in the cool Chicago morning.

Meeting his long stride, she walked beside him into the police station and asked to see Detective Wilson. After being directed to sit in the hardback chairs lining the lobby, they waited nearly twenty minutes before a tall, dark-skinned man in khakis and a blue polo shirt approached them. The logo embroidered on his shirt identified him as part of the Chicago human trafficking task force.

"Ms. Rodriguez?" He held his hand out.

She returned the firm shake and gestured to Dean. "This is my client, and Mandy's brother, Dean Campbell."

"Have you found my sister?" Dean asked.

The detective, hand on Dean's upper arm, gestured toward the door he'd just walked though. "Let's take this to a conference room." He led the way, offering drinks that both Alexa and Dean declined. Once in the room, Detective Wilson sat on one side of a table as Alexa and Dean sat on the other. He looked like a man who had been through this very situation a thousand times. He sat straight, ready to tackle Mandy's case head on, but he also had sympathy in his eyes.

"We traced the number you gave us and arrested the john. He was quick to flip, as they all are. We know which ad he answered and will make a call this afternoon. I want to be clear about one thing. Just because we call the same number doesn't guarantee your sister will be the victim sent to the designated meeting place. He was able to identify her brand, so—"

"Her brand?" Dean asked, looking confused.

Wilson shifted uneasily, but the movement was so slight Dean probably didn't notice. "These girls, they are viewed as property by their exploiters. Property that is marked, usually with tattoos, so other pimps know who the girl belongs to. According to the john, he noticed three stars on her right wrist. Like this." He held up a photo from a stack of papers on his desk, showing them three dark stars outlined on a thin, pale wrist. "This is a brand."

Dean closed his eyes and eased his breath out.

"With Mandy's branding, we've been able to identify her exploiter—"

"Exploiter?" Dean shook his head. "Sorry. I'm just not following."

"We call the men who sell their victims exploiters. These rings aren't old-fashioned prostitution rings, Mr. Campbell. These aren't old-fashioned pimps who take a percentage. These are men who find vulnerable people, usually children or young men and women, find their weakness, and prey on it. These victims are groomed and manipulated into believing they are acting out of love and respect for the person who they perceive to be their protector."

Dean creased his brow. "Are you saying she's been brainwashed?"

"In a sense, yes. We are a lot closer to finding your sister than we were twenty-four hours ago, but that doesn't mean we're that much closer to rescuing her. The fact that she called you is a good sign. She reached out. She wants help. I know this is a horrific situation, but believe me when I tell you that so far she's been lucky."

"Lucky?" Dean snapped. "She's being sold for sex."

Wilson lifted his hand. "But according to the john, she appeared well-fed and healthy. He did indicate that she was taking drugs, but as of two a.m., she was alive and reaching out for help."

"Did he let her use his phone?"

"No. He went to the bathroom. He didn't even know she'd used it." Wilson offered as much reassurance as he could. "We're going to call the ad and set up a sting. Even if Mandy isn't the victim sent to us, as soon as she takes money, we have her and can work on her to turn in her exploiter. Once we get him, we can offer him a deal to turn over all his victims, including Mandy."

"As soon as? Once we?" Dean looked at Alexa, and the desperation in his eyes broke her heart. "Are they even going to find her?"

"We're going to find her," she reassured him. "They break up these rings all the time, Dean. They know what they're doing. They're going to do everything they can to rescue her as soon as possible."

"We know who is selling her, Mr. Campbell. That is more than half the battle here. I want to talk to you about what's going to happen if this is Mandy."

Alexa nodded for him to go ahead. Clearly Dean was not fully focused, but he needed to know there was a plan to save his sister.

"Once she arrives at the room, we have to wait for money to exchange hands before we can consider her activity illegal. Then the officer inside will say the code word to let us know we can make the bust. There will be a survivor advocate with the team. She'll be the one who interacts with Mandy. We're going to find out what drugs she's taking, have her checked by a doctor, and she'll be moved to a recovery center for human trafficking victims."

"She won't come home with me?" Dean asked.

"Unfortunately, we've learned that these women tend to get pulled back into drug abuse, which ultimately leads many of them to return to their pimps. We have to break the cycle, get her clean from her addiction, and get her mentally and emotionally strong enough to resist falling back into this trap."

"How long will that take?"

"It can vary depending on a lot of things. If she wants, we can help her relocate to a recovery center closer to you, but Mr. Campbell, for your sister's sake, it's best that she goes through at least a year of recovery to teach her how to live without drugs and the codependency her exploiter has created."

He sank back, and Alexa put her hand to his arm. "You'll call and let us know if you find Mandy this evening?"

"Of course," he agreed. He focused on Dean. "I'm sorry this happened to your family, Mr. Campbell. But please know, these men are experts at manipulating victims into doing their bidding. This in no way is a reflection of your sister or something she's done. She's a victim of a group of people who have made billions of dollars in human trafficking. She stumbled on the wrong person and was pulled into something she has no way of escaping without help."

"I'm not blaming her," he said.

"There's no way you could have known, either," Alexa assured him. "So stop blaming yourself."

He nodded, but she knew that was about as likely as convincing him to stop breathing.

GETTING DRUNK WASN'T THE ANSWER, BUT DEAN WAS tempted to indulge in the urge anyway. Vomiting hadn't helped. Punching his pillows hadn't helped. Maybe alcohol would ease the sickness settling over his soul. The hotel bar was only two flights down, and the menu on the desk said they offered a wide variety of whiskey. Whiskey would help.

He had just pulled his T-shirt over his head when Alexa knocked on the door. He knew it was her because no one else would be at his door. And because he had that strange knot in his stomach he seemed to get whenever she was near. When he opened the door, his spirits lifted just seeing her there. But they soared when she raised a pizza box and six-pack of beer.

"I was just debating hitting the bar," he confessed, stepping aside.

"I figured." She eyed the bed as she set the pizza and beer on the little table but didn't comment on the disarray of the bedding. His attempt at napping hadn't gone well. The blankets were bunched at the bottom of the bed, and the pillows were piled high against the headboard. "Did you sleep?" she asked, sliding out of her blazer.

"No." In the place where her gun holster usually sat, a sheath held a three-inch blade. "Never without a weapon, huh?"

Hanging her coat on the chair back, she smiled but didn't answer. Lifting the top off the box, she waved her hand like a game show hostess. "I didn't know what you wanted, so I got everything except pepperoni. Gives me indigestion."

He chuckled. "You can eat your grandmother's posole, but pepperoni gives you indigestion."

She grabbed the biggest slice before plopping into a chair. Leaning back, she took a bite, looking as content as either of them possibly could be given the events of the day. "Eat," she said around her mouthful.

"Or you'll tell Abuela?"

"Damn straight."

Sitting on the other side of the little round table, he grabbed a slice as well. But his bites were significantly larger. He finished one slice before she was halfway through hers. Cracking open two beers, he handed her one and chugged from the other.

"Impressive," she said. "Must have made you very popular in college."

Using the back of his hand, he wiped ale from his lips. "That and the underground comics I drew of the professors."

Alexa widened her eyes and turned her lips in an exaggerated and incredibly tempting O shape. "That sounds absolutely mutinous."

A good five seconds passed before he processed her teasing words. He was too caught up in staring at her mouth. "It was *so* mutinous. I almost got kicked out of school, but no one could ever one hundred percent prove it was me."

"Wouldn't have taken you for the bad-boy type, Mr. Campbell."

Giving her a wicked smile, he wriggled his brows. She giggled, and the sound soothed his soul. He made it through a second slice of pizza as she polished off the crust of her first. Leaning back in her chair, she put her hand to her stomach and sipped from the bottle in front of her.

"Is that all you're eating?" he asked, checking out the slices to determine which would be his third.

"I have to let it settle before I decide. Overeating isn't because the stomach isn't full; it's because by the time the stomach recognizes it's full, the body has consumed more than necessary."

"Very scientific." He chose the smallest slice that remained in the box. "Here. Eat this one."

She was clearly going to challenge him but accepted. "Thank you." She nibbled with much less gusto than she'd tackled the first slice with.

He didn't mind. He was glad he wasn't eating alone. "Did you go to college?"

"I have an associate's in criminal justice. Everything else I learned was hands-on from Holly and Eva. We're all still learning, really. Each of us brings something so different to the table, we round the team out in a lot of ways."

"I know you miss Lanie," he said, picking an onion off his pizza, "but it's got to be nice to have family in your coworkers. They'll never replace her, but I'm sure it helps fill the void."

"It does," she said quietly, as if admitting it was something to be embarrassed about. "I love my team. I don't know that I'd stay sane without them." She reached across the table and put her hand on his. "I'm sorry you're going through this alone."

Turning his palm up, he wrapped his fingers around hers. "I'm not. You're here, right? That's what you keep saying, anyway."

She offered him that sweet, supportive smile of hers as she returned his delicate hold. "I am here. Whatever you need."

Something in the air around them stirred. Though the touch was light, the current that ran from her hand to his was explosive. She seemed to notice it as well. Her smile faltered just a fraction before she forced it back into place. Common sense and probably good manners would dictate that he release her hand, but he didn't. She didn't pull away, either. She lightly ran her thumb over his as she took another bite. Then another, until she had finished her slice and he'd finished his beer.

He wanted to open a second beer, but not at the cost of releasing her hand. Finally, though, she pulled back, and he let her go. As much as he wanted to cling to her soft hand, he'd likely made her feel awkward enough. But after opening two beers, Alexa put her hand on his again. As if on cue to interrupt the moment, her phone rang. The oxygen in the room seemed to evaporate. Apprehension made him feel as if he were about to be sick.

"Alexa Rodriguez," she answered.

Holding Dean's gaze, she listened for a moment before shaking her head. "Thanks for letting me know." She ended the call and dropped her phone on the table. "Mandy didn't show."

He exhaled, his shoulders sagging, and dragged a hand down his face.

"I'm sorry. They're going to try again tonight. Are you okay?" she asked.

"No. Not really," he answered honestly. "I'm scared for her. Not just what she's going through but how she's ever going to recover. Mentally, physically, emotionally. How will she ever get over this?"

"With the proper help from qualified professionals and a lot of support from her big brother." She put her other hand on his, making a sandwich of their palms. "This is not going to be easy, Dean. I'm not going to pretend that it will be. She's going to have so many dragons to slay. All you can do is be there to help her when she needs you."

"I will be." Surprised by a spike of emotion, he cleared his throat and shook his head. "Do you think... I mean, after she's home..."

"What?" she pressed.

Tightening his hold on her hand, he met her gaze as he whispered, "Even after she's home, do you think you can help me through this?"

"Yes. Always."

Dean was on his feet and pulling her to hers without thinking. She was tucked in his arms, his chin resting on her head, before he even recognized his actions. He didn't pull away, however, because her arms wrapped around him as well. She stroked his back as she quietly muttered words of reassurance.

"She'll survive this," she said. "We just have to get her home."

Hugging her even more tightly, he inhaled her sweet scent and the beer on her breath. Her heat seeped through his skin, warming the cold that had settled in his soul. He didn't want to release her, but again common sense told him he should. He wouldn't deny that he found Alexa attractive, and not just physically. He also wouldn't deny that he was feeling emotionally broken. Her close proximity seemed to be like dangling a bone in front of a dog and expecting it to sit.

Pulling back, he muttered his apology under his breath, and she told him she didn't mind just as quietly. Exhaling, he snagged his beer and stepped away from her. There weren't a lot of places to sit in the small hotel room, so he dropped on the edge of the bed and leaned against the headboard. Taking a drink, he watched her busy herself with putting the top on the box and wiping her hands.

With her beer in her hand, she sat on the foot of the bed. "If the girl who answers the ad the detective listed is your sister, I want you to be prepared, Dean. She may not be ready to come home with us for several reasons. Embarrassment and shame being only two of them."

"If she chooses to stay here, I'll come here, too. I won't leave her alone again."

"She may not want your support. If that's the case, no matter how challenging it is, you are going to have to step back and give her space, trusting that the counselors can help her." Dropping her hand on his ankle, she squeezed tenderly, her heat seeping into his skin in the gap between his jeans hem and low-cut sock. "You may not be the help that she needs right away. If that's the case, know that she'll turn to you eventually. Just stand back, be strong, and be there when she's ready."

"You've seen this before?"

"Not exactly a case like this, but similar enough that I know young women who have been abused are hesitant to lean on family members who they fear will judge or be disappointed in them. That seems to be tenfold when the family member is male."

"She's not going to trust me."

Her hand moved up his shin, rubbing up and down, lightly stroking as she tried to reassure him. "It isn't about you. Please remember that. Whatever she is going through now and whatever she goes through when she comes back is not about you. You didn't do anything to cause this, and you can't be the one to save her from the damage this has done to her. The only thing you can do, the best thing you can do, is wait and listen and take your cues from her. Don't try to tell her what she needs or how she should heal. Survivors of this type of abuse have suffered in ways you can't possibly understand. Telling them to get over it or trust you or believe in you are just words that mean nothing to them. She's probably going to be more comfortable with women."

"You?"

That damn sweet smile curved her lips. "I'll do whatever she needs me to do." She looked at her hand and jerked it back, as if she hadn't realized what she was doing. Her tan cheeks took on a shade of crimson that made his heart beat a little faster. She was already pretty, with her olive-tinted skin and big brown eyes. The blush creeping up her face highlighted her cheekbones and straight nose.

Again, he moved without considering his actions. He slid to her and gripped her hands so she couldn't leave, as he suddenly feared she'd do. "She doesn't have strong women in her life. Not like you. Mom was a hard worker, but she never really stood up for herself. Mandy needs to learn how to be tough. Like you."

"It will take time to rebuild her confidence, but she can get there. With patience and encouragement. I'll help her."

"And you'll help me not push her too hard."

Caressing his cheek, she whispered, "Yes. You can do this, Dean."

He was going to kiss her. Some crazy primal urge drowned out the logic warning him against it. Lowering his gaze, he stared at her lips.

"I should go," she announced. Dropping her hand, she stood and started for the door as if the room around her were on fire and she needed to escape.

In a sense it was, but her need to run away left him with a storm of disappointment until she stopped halfway across the small room and turned to face him.

"I...I need my coat. My key is in my coat." She marched with a determined gait to the table, snatched her coat, and then looked at him again. "Dean, I like you. You're a great guy, and you're going through a lot right now. Your emotions are understandably all over the place, and..."

He hopped up and stood directly in front of her. "And maybe when the dust settles, this undeniable attraction between us won't be as strong?"

Opening her mouth, she started to speak, but the words seemed to fail her. "Well..."

"Because I don't see that happening."

"You're my client and—"

"You're fired," he stated.

Her eyes widened. "Excuse me?"

"For tonight." Wrapping his arm around her lower back, he pulled her against him. "I'll hire you again in the morning."

"This is unethical," she whispered.

"Not if I've fired you." He brushed her long hair from her forehead, pinning it behind her ear. "You've had days to work on this case, Ms. Rodriguez, and all you've done is everything I couldn't in the last month. I'm not sure I can justify keeping your services with a work record like that. I need time to consider my options."

A smile played across her lips. "You're emotionally distraught right now. I would be taking advantage of you. Once Mandy is home, if you want to see me socially, then...you have my number."

Point taken. He released his hold on her, but she didn't

step around him. She stared up at him, leaving him to debate his next move.

"If you don't want me to kiss you," he said, "you should go."

She hesitated. And he took that as his answer. Cupping her head, he held her as he crashed his mouth to hers.

8

ALEXA WAS ON FIRE. She had no doubt that flames were licking over her skin, heating her flesh to the point of melting. And her mouth, where Dean's lips were pressed against hers? That was the start of the inferno consuming her. In all her time doing this job, she'd never crossed the line into inappropriate behavior with a client, never even considered it. However, *not* crossing the line into inappropriate behavior with Dean didn't seem to be an option.

She parted her lips, all but begging him to delve deeper. His tongue plunged desperately into her mouth as he hugged her against him in a move that would undoubtedly lead to combustion and their ultimate demise. She decided that wasn't such a bad way to go. Fisting his shaggy hair, she returned his passion, moving her tongue over his and nipping at his lip when he pulled away to breathe.

He whispered something about her tasting better than

he'd thought, but Alexa didn't pay much attention. She was distracted by the erection pressing against her stomach as she brushed her nose along the whiskers covering his jaw. They'd left home in the middle of the night and hadn't rested since. The scruff looked good on him and heightened her senses as his coarse hair pricked her skin. There was no longer the hint of minty aftershave that she usually smelled on him. Now there was just the scent of his skin. She liked it. She liked it too much. Rolling her eyes closed, she moaned as she rubbed her cheek over his. She wanted to feel the roughness of his face on every inch of her.

Sinking her teeth into his earlobe, she bit, scraping her teeth over his skin and then sucking away any pain she might have inflicted. He whispered again, this time something about Jesus having mercy on him, which made her smile.

"Are you sure you want this?" she breathed in his ear.

He lifted and turned in one swift movement. Alexa was on her back on the bed before she could object. Not that she would. Pressing her head into the cool pile of sheets, she gasped as he stretched over her, his body fitting perfectly between her legs. His hands seemed to be everywhere at once, squeezing her breast, cupping her ass, pulling her thighs around him. She gripped his hair, guiding his hot mouth over her neck, down to the exposed flesh in the V of her neckline. She started working on releasing the buttons of her shirt as his prickly chin lit her skin on fire, and then he soothed her with licks and kisses.

She'd barely gotten three buttons undone before Dean had the material pushed aside and cupped her breast. She wished she'd worn something sexier than the nude satin cover. He didn't seem to care. He pulled the top of the basic bra down and latched on to her nipple, flicking and nipping as his whiskers scraped her skin.

She pulled his head even closer. "Don't ever shave again," she muttered.

"Hmm?"

She shuddered as the vibration rolled through her over-sensitized skin. Arching her back up, she pulled him even closer. "Your whiskers are everything."

A quiet laugh left him before he deliberately rubbed his chin over her tightened nipple. She hissed, bucked, and smirked when he pushed back, not letting her roll him over. Instead he nipped at her cleavage, licked where he'd bitten, and then moved up to kiss her mouth. Pulling back after thoroughly claiming her mouth, he sat back on his knees between her thighs and pulled his shirt over his head.

She watched him discard the first bit of his clothing.

Rubbing his fingertips over her chest, he gave her a sorrowful look. "Your skin is so red."

"And we're just getting started."

The concern on his face faded into intensity. "Get naked."

"We need a condom."

"On it." He rolled away and grabbed his bag from the luggage rack beside the dresser.

"Somebody had high hopes," she observed as she pulled her shirt off.

"I'm a guy. We always have high hopes." He found what he was looking for and toed off his shoes as he tossed a small packet onto the bed.

By the time she'd unzipped her boots and pulled them free, he was on his knees in front of her, releasing her belt. She held back the urge to tell him how good he looked in the position. Instead she ran her fingers through his hair, anticipating his next move. Her pants hadn't even hit the floor before he gently shoved her back onto the bed. He tugged at her pants, tossed them aside, and used her legs to pull her to the edge of the bed.

Her breath left her in a quivering rush at the feel of his rough stubble pressing between her legs. The heat of his mouth and the softness of his tongue was such a stark contrast, the onslaught of sensations nearly blew her mind. His chin and cheeks burned and pricked. His mouth warmed and stroked. And in response, her muscles almost instantly tensed. Inhaling became nearly impossible.

Gripping the blanket, she moaned and panted and hissed until her eyes rolled back in her head. She was damn near climaxing when he shoved her thighs open wider, clamped down her clitoris, and shoved his fingers inside her. Fireworks exploded behind her eyes. She ground her teeth together as every muscle in her body tensed. She didn't get a chance to relax before he gripped her hips and flipped her over. Panting, she didn't resist as he lifted her to her feet and pressed her shoulders down so her face was in the bed as her ass was aimed in the air for the taking.

Gasping, she clamped her teeth into her lip and listened to the sound of the little foil packet being torn open. Her anticipation built as the distinct sound of latex unrolling hit her ears. She jolted at the feel of Dean's hand between her legs, fingering her, testing her readiness. She was ready. Sweet freaking hell, she was ready. He rubbed his finger over her clit, and she mewed.

Leaning up just enough to look over her shoulder at him, she smirked. "I don't do submissive often, big boy. You'd better take this while you can."

That was all the invitation he needed. The next moment, he lunged forward, and she grunted at the feel of him filling her. He pulled back, slammed forward, until he found a hard and fast rhythm. Oh. Hell. Yes. She loved a man who wasn't afraid to be a little rough with her.

Rotating her hips, she angled her body so he went as deep as nature would allow. He grunted and started moving faster. Reaching between her legs, Alexa found the little magic button he'd spent the last few minutes licking and nipping. Already alert, the bundle of nerves instantly responded to her touch, causing her entire body to tighten.

"Alexa," Dean moaned. "Holy shit."

Between her fondling and his thrusting, her body was ready to explode again. The feel of his hand gripping her hair, gently but firmly tugging the strands, was the last bit of sensation she could handle. Her body had barely stopped quivering when Dean gently shoved her away from him. Falling onto her back, she panted as he stood over her.

He let out a heavy breath as well. "I need like five seconds to calm down, or you're going to be very disappointed in me."

Giggling, she scooted up on the bed until her head rested on one of the pillows. She took advantage of his break to catch her breath and finally see what he had to offer. Little patches of dark hair circled his flat nipples, and a patch started just at his belly button before traveling lower. A band was tattooed around his right bicep, some tribal thing that he probably had no idea of the meaning—if it actually had one—but looked sexy as hell.

Licking her lips, she moaned her appreciation of his body as he huffed out one more breath. Crooking her finger, she silently ordered him to join her. As he moved up the bed, she parted her legs, and he honored her silent request. He didn't taste her with as much gusto as he had a few minutes before, but she didn't mind. In fact, she liked that he was taking his time now, being more attentive and less starved. But she wouldn't complain about either approach.

Dropping her head back, she muttered how good it felt having him there, and he muttered how good it felt to be there. Even so, he moved up her body, kissing her belly, her breasts, and then her neck. He slid into her body much easier this time, with a gentle progression as he moved over her. She let him love her sweetly for a few minutes—that definitely wasn't her style, and when she'd tolerated all the cordial sex she could handle, she rolled him over and straddled his hips. "Making love is great in theory..."

"In theory?"

"This"—she braced her hands on his shoulders for leverage—"is so much better."

Dean gripped her hips and helped her as she started grinding. Together, they found a fast pace that suited them both. She rotated as he lifted, joining their bodies in a way that made her breath catch with each thrust. They fit together perfectly, and not just physically; there was a connection between them, and when she opened her eyes and looked into his, she knew he felt it as well. Leaning down, she brushed his hair from his forehead and kissed him hard as he kept their rhythm without missing a thrust.

"You're right," he said, shoving his body into hers. "This is so much better."

She smiled as she raked her fingers over his strands again. "I'm glad you agree." She licked his lips before leaning back up. Taking his hands from her hips, she put them to her breasts and encouraged him to squeeze. As he did, she moved over him, stroking him with her inner walls, building up the heat between them until it once again threatened to consume her.

"Are you ready?" she asked as the friction built and his grunting increased.

"Ready."

"Brace yourself," she said with a grin and leaned back, resting her hands on his legs. Moving in a fast circle, she gasped at the feel of his hand on her clit as they moved. Yeah, that was the last bit she needed. Slamming her body against his, she once again cried out. This time, he joined her.

Falling forward, breathless and limp, Alexa rested her head next to Dean's. His arms wrapped around her, hugging her tight against his chest. Running his fingers through her hair, he let a long breath leave him.

"Sorry," he whispered.

"For what?"

"Pulling your hair."

She grinned. "Did I complain?"

"I should have asked first."

"Such a gentleman," she said teasingly as she slid off him. "Wash my back, and we'll call it even."

DEAN RAN HIS FINGERTIP DOWN THE DIP IN ALEXA'S back, tracing her spine. Her skin was as soft as satin and had him mesmerized. He couldn't stop touching her. When they'd showered, he washed her back three times and her legs twice. He lost count of how many times he'd washed her breasts. Enough that she'd laughed and told him they were cleaner than they'd ever been. Then he'd covered her in the lemon-scented, hotel-provided lotion.

He couldn't stop touching her now that she'd given him permission. Brushing his lips over her shoulder, he was careful not to press too hard. Despite her insistence that she didn't mind his whiskers, her skin said different. She'd been bright red in all the places he'd kissed, her flesh irritated from his whiskers.

He thought she was asleep until she sighed and muttered into the pillow. He soothed his palm over her back and hushed her. "Sorry. I didn't mean to wake you," he whispered.

"You didn't."

She rolled over lazily, one sluggish motion at a time, and he smiled. He'd never seen her move so clumsily. Brushing her hair from her face, he leaned over her, watching as she licked her lips and blinked several times, as if her mind was slowly rebooting. Her hand fell to his arm as she attempted her normal soothing strokes. Now they were more like heavy pets. Even half asleep, she was trying to comfort him.

Jesus, she was perfect.

Kissing her lightly, he tucked her closer to him. "Close your eyes."

"Are you okay?" she asked.

He didn't answer. He didn't want to lie and say that he was, but he didn't want to disturb her sleep more than he had. Having her warmth seeping into his body was the best thing she could do for him right now, and she didn't have to lose sleep to do that.

Rolling onto her side, clearly more aware, she snuggled into his chest and wrapped her arm around him. Placing a light kiss on his chest, she burrowed deeper. "Talk to me," she whispered.

"There's nothing new to say. My sister is still missing. She's still out there. She's still being sold." He closed his eyes as she stroked his skin, her touch more like her normal comforting strokes than her tired petting. He hadn't realized how much he'd come to rely on those little brushes of her hand. Wrapping her more tightly in his arms, he kissed her head. "I'm scared for her, Lex."

"I know." She stroked her soothing hand over his arm. "I wish I could do more."

"You've done so much." Kissing her head, he hugged her even closer. "It's in the hands of the police now. You made that happen. They wouldn't listen to me. I just wish this was over. For her and me. And, yes, I know that sounds selfish when she's the one really suffering."

"Hey, you've suffered, too. Believe me, I know how hard it is. No, it's not the same hell she's going through, but it's still hell, and you are allowed to hope for it to end for your sake, too."

She stroked his cheek, and he had to smile. He definitely would be keeping the facial hair that seemed to have her so enthralled. Taking her hand in his, he kissed her fingertips, silently thanking whatever force had brought her to him.

He'd been slowly losing his mind since he'd realized Mandy had disappeared. He'd foolishly thought that he'd survived raising his sister and had patted himself on the back for a job well done. He now understood what his mother had meant all those times she'd insisted that just because he was grown didn't mean her job was done. He'd never be done helping Mandy find her way through life. He just hoped to God he'd get the chance to see her through this. Alexa's warning that Mandy might reject his help hadn't stopped bouncing through his mind.

"Dean?" Alexa whispered, pulling his mind back to her.

"Sorry. My mind keeps wandering. Did Detective Wilson give any indication when he might call back?"

"No. Try to sleep, hmm?"

"Not much chance of that." Untangling himself from her arms, he sat up and put his feet to the floor. Running his hands through his hair, he was reminded yet again that he was due for a haircut. Digging his fingers into his eyes, he exhaled loudly. "You should rest, though. It's getting late."

The crisp sheets rustled as she moved. A moment later, her warmth surrounded him. Her chest pressed against his back, skin on skin, and she slithered her arms around him. She rested her cheek against his shoulder. "I can't rest when you're so upset."

"Then you may never rest again." Closing his eyes, he focused on the feel of her lips pressing against him, once more confused by her ability to ease his stress with a simple touch. But as her hand lowered, her touch was anything but simple. Enchanting. Seductive. Molten. Inhaling as she wrapped her long fingers around his erection, Dean rolled his head back and moaned.

His body heated instantly, his ability to breathe halted, and his troubles faded. Nothing in the world existed except the steady up-and-down movement of her hand. She seemed to be able to read his mind for exactly how fast to move, how hard to squeeze, how far to take him before slowing and easing her hold. Then she'd start again, masterfully enticing his soul to follow her wherever she led him.

Like the mystical creature he was beginning to think she was, she effortlessly moved around to straddle his legs. Gripping her waist, helping her balance, he inhaled as much as his lungs would hold. He was lost. He was help-lessly lost in everything about this woman. And that was a blessing.

More than a blessing, he realized, when her other hand reached down and caressed his balls as she rhythmi-cally stroked. And her mouth. Fuck, he was falling in love with her mouth. She sank her teeth into his lip, just hard enough to remind him there was more to his body than his crotch. He moved his hand higher and rubbed the ball of his thumb over her nipple until the nub pebbled. Once it was hard against his touch, he pinched and tugged. His reward was a sharp breath hissing from between her teeth. He licked her mouth before covering his lips with his, kissing her until he was breathless.

"Hey," she whispered. "I'm taking care of you."

"Yes, you are."

A sultry laugh left her throat and rolled through him like a wildfire through dry timber. Grabbing a condom off the nightstand beside him, he handed it to her, holding his breath as she unrolled it over his erection. Slipping his arms under her knees, Dean held her as he rolled their bodies. He had her back against the mattress and her knees pressed to her shoulders before she could agree or protest. She did neither. She simply grinned, clearly pleased by his bold move.

She hadn't told him that she liked rough sex, but the cues she was putting off seemed to indicate she didn't mind it. Even so, after kissing her, he whispered, "Tell me if I get too out of hand."

Her grin widened. "You tell me if I get too out of hand."

With her pinned between the bed and his body, Dean thrust into her. She exhaled with a pant and closed her eyes as he found that same hard, fast rhythm they'd used before. Only now she gripped his hair, tugging hard enough to add to his overall sensations. No wonder she hadn't complained when he'd tugged hers. The touch of pain increased his pleasure tenfold.

"You feel so fucking good," he grunted out, grinding into her.

"Mmm," she moaned out. "Harder."

Digging his toes into the mattress, he used the leverage to drive himself into her hot body. She shifted as well, rolling her hips up to meet him in a motion that nearly drove him insane with pleasure. Some strange noise—a cross between a scream and a grunt and a prayer of thanks —erupted from him as she dug her nails in his back and dragged them over his flesh. Her nails weren't long, he'd noticed that from all the times he'd stared at her hand on his arm as she comforted him, but long enough that he was confident she'd just left long welts down his back.

The image that formed in his mind of the mark she'd left on him spoke to that primal part that she seemed to awaken deep inside him. He wanted to howl at the moon when he was inside her. He wanted to smell every inch of her, memorizing the woman that his soul had claimed as his. He'd never felt such a strong connection to another person. Not just another lover, but another human being. There was something here that reached him on the most basic level; it seemed too simple, too right, to make sense. But it made perfect sense.

Latching his mouth to hers, Dean dipped his tongue into her mouth as she clutched his head between her palms and met his kiss with as much heat and passion as their bodies created while moving together. Her muscles tensed around him and a deep grunt rose from inside her, sending him over the edge with her. He pulled her to him, plunged one more time into her depths, and joined her as she let the sensations take complete control of her mind and body.

[9]

ALEXA DREW her lungs full of air, and the scent of coffee dragged her from the fog of sleep. Taking another deep breath, she confirmed that someone was brewing a pot of life's sweetest gift. Stretching, she lifted her eyelids and instantly smiled at the bare-assed man watching the individual-serving pot drain into a paper cup. He muttered and put his hands on his hips, clearly frustrated at the little machine.

Rolling onto her side, she propped her head on her hand and took her time skimming over his naked figure. Toned calves and thighs led to a tight ass that flexed as he leaned forward a bit, watching the coffee brew. The muscles in his back weren't defined until he moved, and they bulged under his lightly freckled skin. What drew her attention, though, were the bright red scratches that went from his shoulders to about halfway down to his hips.

Whoops.

She grinned, not really sorry at all. He'd liked the feel of her nails dragging down his back. He'd liked that a lot. Her cheeks warmed at the memory of how he'd become even more alive at the bit of pain she'd inflicted. She hadn't meant to, especially to the point of leaving marks, but he'd felt so fucking good moving inside her. She could probably spend the rest of her life in bed with this man and never regret it.

"Fucking thing," he whispered under his breath.

She nibbled her lip as she soaked in how adorable he looked cursing at a single-pot coffee machine while standing there naked as the day he was born. Even so, she didn't see any point in prolonging the obvious. "There's a coffee shop right across the street. Not only is the coffee better, but the servings are much larger. That cup doesn't hold enough to keep a flea awake."

Dean glanced over his shoulder and pressed his lips into a scowl. "Going across the street certainly would have been faster." He glared at the cup one more time before giving up and returning to bed. Cupping her head, he tasted her mouth before hopping off the bed and snagging the bag that held his clothes. "You take it black, right?"

"Give me a minute and I'll go with you."

He dropped his bag on the bed and started sorting through the contents. "I really need to up my game if you have the ability to walk across the street after last night."

Alexa fell onto her back as she laughed. "Oh, honey. You're good. But I'm stronger than the average female."

Something reminiscent of admiration found his lips. "I

see the bar is high. Don't fret. I'm dedicated to reaching it."

"I have no doubt," she said sincerely. He'd more than proven he was an attentive lover. Even so, she was excited by his commitment to try harder. She pushed herself up and watched him staring at her breasts as she moved to him. Stopping in front of him, she slid her palms up his arms and around his shoulders. "I'm looking forward to your efforts."

He hugged her tight as he tasted her lips. "Not nearly as much as I am. Get dressed. I need coffee, and then I want to go back to the police station. I want an update on where they are with looking for Mandy."

She instantly felt a bit deflated. Not because he wanted to go look for his sister but because Alexa knew he would be disappointed by whatever news he received. Had the police found Mandy, Detective Wilson would have called. Dean's sister was still out there, likely sleeping off a night of selling her body in exchange for food and drugs from some pimp who treated her like property instead of a person. Mandy's situation hadn't changed overnight. And might not change for a very long time.

Brushing her hand over Dean's stubble, she held his gaze. "We're going to find her. We will. But it might not be as easy as you're hoping."

His eyes saddened. "I know that. But you've brought us this close to her. I believe we'll find her. I have to believe it will be sooner rather than later. For her sake."

"I hope so. I just don't want you counting on something that might not happen. You know, when we find her—"

He cut her off with a quick kiss. "I woke up feeling hopeful for the first time in as long as I can remember. Maybe it's foolish to cling to that, but I'm going to. For a while anyway. Okay?"

"Okay," she whispered.

"Get dressed. Let's grab some coffee and something to eat. Then I want a quick shower before we go see what the police have to tell us."

Though she knew that if the human trafficking unit had anything new, they would have gotten a call, she let him cling to that little bit of hope that he'd mentioned as she made herself presentable enough to run to the coffee shop.

Though Holly and Jack tended to keep their PDA to a minimum, Eva and Josh weren't above holding hands or sharing a quick kiss in front of the rest of HEARTS. Alexa had always envied their affection, so when Dean grabbed her hand the moment they were outside the hotel room, she very nearly swooned. She thought she looked like hell with her messy bun, wrinkled clothes, and freshly washed face, but as they waited for the elevator, he put his arm around her shoulder, kissed her temple, and told her she looked beautiful.

She believed him. Not because she thought so but because his whispered words snaked down and hugged her heart and lifted her spirits, despite the reality of why they were in Chicago. A sense of guilt settled low in her stomach, but she ignored it. Being with Dean didn't take one bit of effort away from her determination to find his sister. In fact, she felt even more determined this morning.

She needed to fix this for him. She needed to take this burden from his shoulders and know what he was like when he was happy and whole. She needed to save his sister to help him feel complete. So, yes, her determination was even stronger. But her dread was stronger as well. Finding Mandy didn't guarantee a happy ending for her or for Dean. Alexa knew how difficult it was for trafficking victims to recover from the tools used to hold them captive —whether it was drug addiction or psychological abuse, the hold pimps tended to have over their victims was hard to break.

Oftentimes, even after sobering up or receiving treatment, the women found themselves falling back into the pattern of trafficking. After a while, it was all they knew, and even though it was dangerous and abusive, the cycle pulled them back. Alexa prayed Mandy was strong enough to resist the pull of that life once she was out.

The jingle of the bell above the coffee shop door and the aromas inside helped ease some of the darkness looming in Alexa's mind. As they looked over the menu, her stomach growled, and Dean made a dramatically astonished face, making her laugh. Again, despite the circumstances, she felt being with him like that was right. Perfect.

They'd placed their order and moved aside to wait for their food and drinks before reality crashed down on them.

She actually sensed the shift in Dean's mood before she noticed the gloom clouding his eyes. Lifting her gaze to his face, she swallowed hard at the sudden change in his mood. Following whatever had him enthralled, and suddenly depressed, she read the poster he was fixated on.

Over the image of a girl, probably not much older than Mandy, big bold letters stated that human trafficking wasn't a third-world problem and to call the phone number at the bottom to report suspected abuse. Stepping in front of him, blocking his view, she waited for him to finally see her instead of looking through her.

"How could I have let this happen to her?" he asked under his breath.

"You couldn't have known."

"I *should* have known. She's my sister."

"Who was away at college." She glanced at the barista, who'd called her name. "Can you make those sandwiches to go?" she asked.

The girl barely concealed her eye roll before taking the tray back to wrap the sandwiches and drop them in a bag. Alexa wasn't sure if she should add to the tip for the extra work or subtract for the dramatic response, but she only debated for a moment before focusing on Dean again.

Lightly touching his face, she offered him as much of a supportive smile as she could manage. "There is no one to blame but the person who pulled her into whatever mess she's in. Someone out there saw a vulnerable young woman and took advantage of her instead of helping her. That is where the blame falls. That is who we are going to make sure pays for what's happened to her. It's not your fault. Or hers. She is the victim here, and you had no way of knowing what was happening to her."

"I appreciate what you're saying." He tucked her hair behind her ear. "I really do. But I can't help but feel that I failed her."

"I know," she said. "And I can't stop you from feeling that. But I want you to hear me when I tell you that you couldn't have prevented this."

"You don't know that," he muttered as he turned away. He reached the counter just as the disgruntled barista dropped a bag on the counter. Alexa dug a few extra dollar bills from her pocket and set them on the counter next to the paper coffee cups with their drinks. Taking the cups, she followed Dean from the shop and across the street. The affection he'd displayed just a few minutes earlier was gone, but Alexa didn't blame him. The poster had plucked at the desperation constantly hanging over his head. She understood. She sympathized. She'd been there.

Years had passed before she could see or hear the word *sisters* without feeling like her heart was being obliterated. *Sisters.* Such a simple but powerful word. A word that made her feel less than whole even now. Lanie was gone. Her sister was gone. A part of her soul was gone.

Forever, it seemed.

She wouldn't let that happen to Dean. He might feel this burden now, but she'd be damned if he felt it forever, as she would.

Quickening her stride to keep his pace, she walked beside him back to his hotel room.

"I'm sorry," he said as he pulled their breakfast from the bag. "I didn't mean to spoil the morning."

"Spoil the morning?" Resting her palm to his arm, she sighed. "You didn't spoil anything."

"We were both in such a good mood before..."

"Hey." She moved closer, demanding that he look into her eyes. "We're here for Mandy. I know that. I don't resent that in any way. Do you understand?"

He licked his lips. "What happened between us last night..."

Alexa's heart nearly stopped beating. She didn't want to hear what she was certain he was going to say. She didn't want him to feel like she was a mistake. If he regretted making love to her, she'd probably shrivel and die from humiliation. Not that she'd never been rejected before; she had plenty of times, just as she'd rejected men plenty of times. Something about what she'd shared with Dean was different, though. She'd felt a connection to him that she'd never felt before, and if he hadn't...that would hurt. Deeply.

He let out a long breath. "Alexa, I don't want you to think last night was just a fling or just me being emotional. We don't know each other well, but I like you. A lot. And last night was amazing. It's just this shit with Mandy has my mind so boggled."

Disappointment hit her like a fist to the gut. "And getting involved with me is too much. I get it."

"What? No. That's not what I'm saying." Sliding his arm around her waist, he pulled her against him and pressed his other hand to her cheek. "I just meant that this morning should be about us, about us connecting, but I can't stop thinking about Mandy."

Alexa felt a bit ashamed at how much relief washed over her. Covering his hand with hers, she kissed his palm. "Finding Mandy *should* be your priority, Dean. Don't feel bad about that. Honestly, if your sister wasn't at the forefront of your mind, I'd be worried about your character." Stroking his hand, she tried to ease the concern in his eyes. "Your sister is the most important thing. As she should be."

He sighed and pulled her close for a hard but fast kiss. "Thank you for understanding."

"Of course."

Funny how her heart was racing. Not from the kiss but from the fear that had struck her at the idea of him ending something that hadn't even really begun. She wasn't sure if that was because she was so certain of the connection she felt to him or if she was so desperate to have a taste of what Holly and Eva had found that she was putting more stock in having sex with Dean than she should. The downside of being the emotional member of the HEARTS team was just that—she was too emotional sometimes.

The other women were analytical about things like this. Holly had picked her emotions apart before deciding she loved Jack. Eva had held Josh at arm's length until she was certain. Rene and Tika didn't seem interested in romance, and Sam didn't seem to struggle moving in and out of relationships. Alexa felt things more deeply, which made her second-guess what her heart was feeling now.

She could fall for Dean hard and fast if she allowed herself. But that didn't make it real. He could very well just be reaching out to her because she was there. The thought saddened her beyond reason, but now wasn't the time to ask him about his feelings or his intentions. If he only needed her body and her tenderness to help him through this, then she was to blame for allowing him to do so. If her heart got broken because she'd allowed herself to fall for a client, that was on her.

He'd made no promises or whispered sweet words to get her into his bed. She'd done so willingly and without expectations. Placing expectations on him, especially with all he was going through, would be unfair. She'd take what he offered and offer what she was willing, but she wouldn't allow herself to fall any deeper until she knew where he stood, and she wouldn't burden him with that question until his sister's disappearance was resolved.

Accepting another quick peck from his lips just gave her one more reason to get to the bottom of this case as quickly as possible.

DEAN TOOK ANOTHER DEEP INHALATION AS THE HEAT in the car stirred Alexa's scent around him. Something had shifted between them last night. Not just the sex, but something deeper. He wanted to tell her that, but the words seemed stuck in his mind. Not because he feared rejection. He could survive that. He feared saying something stupid that would make her not want to work Mandy's case any longer. That would be devastating.

Alexa had come so much closer to finding Mandy than Dean ever would have on his own. He owed her so much. If he hadn't decided to hire her, he never would have guessed Mandy had gotten herself mixed up in this kind of mess. Knowing she really was in trouble wasn't exactly a step in the right direction, but it was better than wondering if she were dead somewhere.

He needed Alexa focused on the case, but he couldn't help but need some of her focus on him, too. What a selfish prick he'd grown up to be. His father was right about him. He was a disappointment.

"Dean?"

He turned at the sound of Alexa's sweet voice. "Huh?"

"Are you okay?"

He frowned as he took another breath, smelling her on the air. "I can smell you."

She glanced over, a smirk on her lips that made his cheeks grow warm.

"I mean..." Sniffing the air, he shrugged. "Your shampoo or body wash or whatever."

"You like it?"

"Yeah."

Her smile widened. "Good. I'd hate for all that sniffing to be a bad thing."

Reaching over, he pulled her right hand from the

steering wheel and kissed it. "It's not a bad thing. I didn't realize I was sniffing, though. Sorry."

"Don't be." She turned her hand over and squeezed his. "We have a few more minutes before we get to the station. Want to tell me what's on your mind?"

"For the sake of transparency?"

"For the sake of you not losing your mind."

He smiled at how perceptive she seemed to be. "I, um... I'm worried that having sex with you will make you regret taking this case. Or having sex with me. I don't want you to regret either."

"I don't." She tightened her hold on him and held his gaze for what was probably as long as she could safely since she was driving. "I don't regret either. Do you?"

"No. If you decide that you do, tell me, okay? I need you trying to find my sister. But I also need you helping me. If that gets to be too much, I'll back off. Mandy needs you more. Okay?"

"I agree." She pulled her hand from his so she could use both hands to turn into the public parking lot outside the police station. Once she parked, she turned in her seat and faced him, looking like he'd answered a question that had been nagging her as well. "Mandy comes first. For both of us. Agreed?"

"Agreed."

She reached across the car and brushed his hair from his forehead. "I like you, Dean. But that won't stand in my way from doing what I'm here to do."

"Good."

"Is that all that's worrying you? Besides the obvious, I mean."

He looked out at the cars around them, not really seeing them. "Besides the obvious, yes."

Stroking his hair in a way that he'd already come to rely on, she soothed the edges of his anxiety. "I'm here for you. Whatever you may be thinking or feeling. I'm here."

"I was thinking about what my father said. How I was too wrapped up in myself to take care of her."

"Don't do that. I don't know what your father's problem is, but I do know you took care of your sister."

"I appreciate that," he said quietly. "But you weren't there. So you can't know. Don't," he said when she opened her mouth as if to argue. "Please. Nothing you say can make this better. I appreciate you trying, though." Leaning across the console, he kissed the corner of her mouth. "Come on. Let's go see if they have anything new to share."

He climbed from the car and waited for her. When she joined him, he took her hand, amazed at the calming effect she had on him. He wasn't anticipating good news. He was smarter than that, even without her warning, but that didn't ease the stress that increased with each step. He needed to hear that Mandy was safe. He didn't need her to come home or agree to his help. He just needed to hear the words *Mandy is safe*.

He didn't expect to.

The look on Detective Wilson's face confirmed that before he even spoke. As soon as Dean and Alexa sat in his office, he dropped into a chair and huffed out his breath. "We are going to keep trying, but I have to tell you there was a lot of movement with the girls overnight."

"What does that mean?" Dean demanded.

"The john who was arrested got out on bail. Soon after, ads started getting pulled and the second meeting we had set up didn't show. Our guess is that the john made a call to the pimp and warned him that we busted him and took the victim into custody. If this pimp is holding true to his past behavior, he's going to be lying low for a few days while he moves his victims around."

"Moves them where?" Alexa asked. The alarm in her tone heightened Dean's concern.

"We don't know for certain. We've got people out there asking questions. We'll keep checking online, but I expect him to be a bit more cautious for the next few weeks."

"Do you think he moved Mandy?"

"No way of knowing."

Dean focused on Alexa. "What's happening?"

Her frown deepened as she met his gaze. "The man who we think is using Mandy has been tipped off. There's a possibility she's no longer in Chicago."

His heart dropped like a brick in a shallow pool, hitting the bottom of his stomach with what he was certain was an audible *thud*. "Where is she? Where would she go?"

Though her touch usually soothed him, when Alexa put her hand to his arm, he pulled back and pushed himself up so he could pace as he raked his fingers through his hair.

"We don't know anything for certain," Detective Wilson said. "We're looking into it. Until we confirm that she's been relocated, we'll keep looking in the greater Chicago area for her."

"How long until you can confirm?" Dean looked from Alexa to the detective and back again. The misery on their faces told him everything they weren't saying. They didn't know. They couldn't know.

Mandy had slipped through their fingers.

"Damn it," Dean cursed and marched toward the door. He didn't answer when Alexa called out to him. This wasn't her fault, he wasn't blaming her, but he needed to get his head around what was happening.

Though he'd known it was a long shot that they would Mandy overnight, he hadn't been expecting to find out that she might be gone again. He wasn't prepared for that. He felt sick. He felt weak. And useless. He was outside in the cool air, taking deep breaths, before Alexa called out to him again.

Turning, he dragged his hand through his hair. "Where is she, Lex?"

"I don't know," she whispered. "Dean, I'm so sorry. We aren't giving up."

"What's happening to her? What's being done to her?"

"Shh," she hushed, putting her hand on his arm. "Don't put yourself through that. Focus on finding her."

"How is she going to survive this?"

Gripping his shoulders, she gave him a gentle shake. "She's going to survive this because she has you. You are going to help her through this. And I am going to help you. Don't shut me out, Dean. Let me help. This is difficult, I know"—she pressed when he tried to look away from her—"but nothing about this has been or is going to be easy."

"I know that. I just..." He swallowed as an unexpected surge of desperation nearly brought him to his knees. "I'm scared for her," he whispered.

"That's okay. But don't let that overwhelm you."

"I don't know what to do." He scraped at his hair again. "I don't know what to do."

She brushed his hair, probably trying to get it under control after his frantic movements. "Let's go back to the hotel. You need to get some rest."

"No."

"You need rest," she insisted.

"*No.*"

"There is nothing more we can do here, Dean."

He pulled back. "I can't sit on my hands and do nothing."

She looked hurt by his refusal, so he looked away, not needing the burden of letting down someone else.

"I don't mean to be harsh."

"You're not," she said. "I understand your frustration, but there is nothing we can do here."

"I can't rest," he said more softly.

Alexa seemed to consider before nodding. "Okay. Come with me."

He followed her back inside and to the front-desk area, where she asked to see the human trafficking advocate. His stomach knotted as he realized he'd almost rather go back to the hotel and sleep than go through whatever Alexa was about to do. He didn't ask her plan because he didn't think he wanted to know.

Several minutes passed before a short, heavyset woman walked out to greet them. She held her hand out to him, and the same kind of tender understanding filled her eyes that he'd come to recognize in Alexa's. He took her hand as she introduced herself as Sandra Cawling, social worker, human trafficking survivor, and the person who was going to treat him to his second cup of coffee of the day.

They walked to the little coffee shop across the street, making small talk that Dean didn't really listen to. Sandra and Alexa talked about work, cases, and weather while Dean trailed behind them. At the coffee shop, three mugs were set in front of them and filled without anyone asking, but the waitress disappeared with the wave of Sandra's hand, making Dean think this was a normal part of the social worker's day.

"This isn't easy," Sandra said. "Seeing a loved one being exploited never is."

Dean looked out the window. He'd definitely made the wrong decision by coming here instead of going back to the hotel.

"Dean is struggling with blaming himself," Alexa said.

He wanted to be angry about her breach of his confidence, but he couldn't be. She was right. He was struggling, and he needed help.

"That's common. My mother still has moments when she breaks down crying when she sees me. I expect that to stop sometime, but I have no idea when." She sipped her drink. "Do you want to know how I got pulled in?"

He did. But he didn't. So he didn't answer.

"I was an outcast at school. No matter what I tried, I didn't fit in. So I withdrew into myself and started spending a lot of time on my computer. I found this group online for people like me. We railed against the in-crowd. We supported each other through being bullied. And one day, one of the *friends* I'd made asked me to send him a picture. I did. He told me I was pretty. I'd never been told that before."

Dean looked at her. She wasn't a model by any means, but Sandra wasn't an ugly woman either. She wouldn't stand out in a crowd for being too attractive or too unattractive. She was average. An everyday person. He couldn't imagine no one had ever told her she was pretty.

She smiled as if she could read his mind. "I was an overweight, pimply teen back then, Mr. Campbell. I'd inadvertently told a predator my weakest point. He knew what I wanted to hear. After a few days, he asked to meet in real life. I did." She laughed, but it was flat as her focus seemed to get lost on the past. "He bought me dinner and talked to me like I was a person. Then he started buying me things like nice clothes and medication for my acne. One day he said he was in trouble and needed money. He said I could help." She blinked several times and focused on Dean again before continuing. "He'd been so kind to me, my only real friend, so of course I wanted to help him. But then he told me *what* he needed me to do."

Dean's stomach knotted. He wanted to tell her to stop, but he couldn't. He needed to hear this, because this could very well be Mandy's story, too.

Sandra sighed loudly. "I didn't want to have sex with his so-called friend, but I didn't want to disappoint the only man who had ever been kind to me. So I closed my eyes tight and pretended to be somewhere else, and I did it. Then I did it again and again. Every time to help my friend who said he was in trouble. I didn't understand that I was being prostituted for two years. I thought I was just helping a man who cared about me."

"Did he drug you? Mandy's been drugged."

"He didn't need to drug me. He knew what I was missing and he gave it to me. In return, I fell into a cycle of human trafficking without understanding what was happening. I was arrested twice before someone sat me down and explained that what I was doing was prostitution. Just because I met men in nice hotel rooms to *help a friend* didn't mean I wasn't being exploited."

Dean shook his head slightly. "Mandy was never bullied. She was popular in school."

"This doesn't just happen to kids who are outcasts.

166 / MARCI BOLDEN

These people know how to find someone's weakness and break them."

Dean lowered his face and drew a breath. "I'm sorry for what you went through."

"And I'm sorry for what you are going through," Sandra said softly. "But this isn't your doing or Mandy's. The world is full of monsters. Unfortunately, one found your sister and pulled her into his web. But she has a hell of a team of people on her side. We're going to find her and help her through this. I know you feel like you're on your own here, but you're not. Neither is she."

When she reached across the table, Dean took her hand. Then he took Alexa's. His guilt hadn't abated, his desperation hadn't eased, but for a moment he let himself soak up their support and once again let himself feel hope that Mandy would come home and somehow, someday, everything would be okay.

10

ALEXA PARKED in Dean's driveway and turned her head to him. Returning home without Mandy had been a huge disappointment for them both. He'd been quiet most of the drive back, but Alexa didn't blame him. She'd warned him that even if they'd found Mandy, she might not return. Even so, the reality of leaving Chicago without her had hit him hard.

"Want me to stay?" Alexa asked.

"Do you want to stay?"

She patted his thigh. "Tell you what. You go in and take a shower and get some rest. I'll swing by around dinnertime."

"With something from Abuela?"

"Most likely."

He smiled for the first time since leaving Sandra at the police station in Chicago. "That'd be good. Thanks."

Her heart sped up in her chest when he leaned over

and kissed her sweetly before climbing from her car. She waited until he was inside before backing out, mostly because she was dreading going into the office. She had about fifteen minutes from the time she left his house until she walked into HEARTS and had to face Holly. Holly would see through her if she tried to hide that she had slept with Dean. There was no point in even trying. Those women could sniff out a secret as easily as they could a slice of chocolate cake hidden in a desk drawer.

No. There was no lying about or denying what had happened in Chicago. Alexa just had to figure out how the fallout was going to go. She wouldn't get fired or reprimanded; that wasn't her concern, but the thought of seeing disappointment in the eyes of her coworkers was even worse than the idea of losing her job. She didn't want them to think less of her, and she feared they would.

Worst-case scenario, really, was that Holly would take her off the case. If she did that, Alexa figured Dean would probably fire the team altogether. He didn't seem interested in working with someone else. They had built a foundation of trust before they'd slept together.

Tapping her fingers on the steering wheel, she let herself dwell on the inevitable conversation as she drove on autopilot to the office. Once she parked, she looked up at the intentionally nondescript one-story building. Everything about HEARTS was intentionally nondescript. No flashy signs, no flashy ads. They kept the business low-key and under the radar for a reason—the less attention they drew to themselves, the easier it was to blend in and not be

noticed, which was highly beneficial for private investigators.

Just over a year ago, Alexa had met her old friends
Holly and Eva for dinner, where they announced they
were joining forces to form a PI agency. Did she want in?
Hell yes, she wanted in. That was everything she'd ever
wanted, and she didn't regret a moment of the hard work
or bonding that had taken place.

Building a company from scratch hadn't been easy.
People—mostly men—weren't always interested in hiring
female investigators, but HEARTS found a way to
survive. And grow. In a few short months, their team grew
into six crazy, mix-and-match personalities that couldn't
be better suited to working together.

She wouldn't lose that. She *couldn't* lose that. Not
that she really thought she would. She thought, or at
least hoped, her teammates would understand that
screwing her client wasn't something she did on a regular
basis. And Dean was...special. As lame as that sounded,
it was true. She felt something for him that she couldn't
explain.

Exhaling a slow breath, she shoved her car door open
and headed inside. "Is Holly in?" she asked as she passed
Sam without any other greeting.

"Well, hello to you, too, buttercup. No, Holly isn't in.
Everyone else is, though."

Alexa headed straight to Rene's office. Rene was a
straight shooter. She could tell her what happened and get
an honest reaction. If Holly was going to be pissed, Rene

would tell Alexa to brace for the ice storm that would befall her.

Knocking as she entered, she offered a weak smile to her teammate. "Busy?"

Rene glanced up. "No, come on in."

Alexa closed the door behind her as she did, and Rene sat a bit higher, clearly taking notice. Doors only closed around here when there was about to be a top-secret conversation.

"What is it?" Rene asked without prompting.

Sitting in the chair across from Rene, Alexa puffed up her cheeks, which warmed as she recalled the feel of Dean's body tangled with hers. She had to say it. Just confess and...

Rene's expression didn't change, but something in her eyes shifted as she slapped the folder on her desk closed. "You fucked him."

Dropping her mouth open, Alexa gasped and then snapped her lips together.

Crossing her arms, Rene leaned them on her desk and stared at Alexa. "Are things awkward now?"

"With you and me or me and Dean?"

Rene narrowed her eyes. "With *our* client."

"No." Alexa hadn't meant for the word to sound like a pout, but it had. "We agreed we wouldn't let our relationship get in the way of finding his sister. Mandy comes first. We agreed."

Rene sat back, looking more disappointed than angry. Alexa had been right in her assessment—disappointing her teammate was much worse than angering her. Her chest ached under the weight.

"I messed up. I know that. But I like him, Rene. I *really* like him."

Her features softened into a rare display of sympathy. "Oh, Lex. This is could be a disaster."

"Are you mad?"

"No, I'm not mad. Do I think screwing him before the case is resolved was stupid? Yes." She sighed but quickly followed the sound with a chuckle. "And I just lost twenty bucks."

Creasing her brow, she let the words process. "What?"

The faux innocence on her face only added to the air of mischief. "Hmm?"

"Why would you have lost..." Gasping dramatically, Alexa widened her eyes. "You guys were betting on whether I would sleep with Dean?"

"Not on if, on when. You blush every time he comes around. We could see that you liked him."

Sinking back, Alexa wasn't sure if *she* should be mad or not but decided her coworkers' gambling habits didn't matter. "I do like him. He's so sweet."

"And he likes you, I assume."

Alexa nodded. "Yeah. I think so."

"I hope so. You deserve to be happy, Lex. But I do have to say, I'm worried that this could end badly."

Alexa shrugged. "Anything can end badly, right?"

Rene lowered her eyes for a moment. "Right. Did you find his sister?"

She shook her head. "Her pimp caught wind that the police had busted one of his johns. He moved his girls before we could find her. But she's on the radar of the human trafficking unit in Chicago, and the detective there is going to send her picture to the heads of other departments. If she gets arrested, he'll be notified and will let me know."

"And if that doesn't happen?"

Alexa knew that was a possibility, but hearing it from Rene made her dread run deeper. Their best bet of finding and rescuing Mandy was for her to be handed over to a social worker after being arrested for prostitution. "I've got a file on her pimp. I'm going to start digging into him."

Rene nodded. "Good. Listen, I don't know what Holly's going to think about you and Dean, but if she wants to reassign the case, I'll take it and make it a priority."

Another possibility she didn't want to face. "Thank you. I appreciate that. Do you know when she'll be back?"

"I don't." She glanced beyond Alexa's head, as if to verify they were alone before leaning forward and speaking with a softer tone. "Something is off with her."

Alexa lowered her gaze.

"You know what it is," Rene accused.

Meeting her eyes again, Alexa nodded. "I can't talk about it, but, yes, she's working through something."

Concern like Alexa had never seen filled Rene's eyes. "Is she sick?"

"No," Alexa quickly said. "No. Nothing like that.

She's fine. She and Jack are fine. It's...something else, nothing..." She pressed her lips together, knowing she had to give Rene an answer without breaching Holly's trust. "She might have a new lead on an old case. One that's not what she expected."

Rene didn't seem appeased, but she didn't press for more. "Are you helping her with this old case?"

"No. But I've offered." She ground her teeth together, considering her words before speaking. "I've suggested she bring this case to the team, but it's a bit personal for her, and she feels that it is her responsibility to solve it."

"Holly feels sole responsibility for something. Imagine that."

Alexa smiled. "Yes, imagine." Pushing herself up to prevent herself from saying too much, she blew out her breath. "Thanks for offering to be my backup on this case, Rene. I hope it doesn't come to that, but if it does, we'll sit down and go over everything more closely."

"Alexa," she called. "You're a good investigator. But you're human too, and it's okay to share your burdens. Remember that."

"We all need to remember that," she said before leaving. Though she was exhausted and had a perfectly good reason to go straight home, she wanted to sort through her e-mail and any other messages that had landed on her desk. However, after a quick skim of her inbox didn't show a single bit of new information being offered on Mandy's whereabouts, Alexa realized that she had little interest in anything else. She deleted some junk mail and sat back in her chair, letting her eyes swim as she considered the facts she had in Mandy's case. Before long, as her mind tended to do, she was thinking about Lanie.

Opening the bottom drawer of her desk, she grabbed the worn manila folder that had long ago started to fray along the edge where she had picked it up time and time again. Setting the folder on her desk, she flipped the top open and was greeted with an old eight-by-ten photo of her sister. The image was permanently burned into Alexa's mind, so much so that she sometimes saw the picture when she closed her eyes at night.

She set the photo aside and read the police report that she'd memorized years ago. The next page in the file was the typed notes Alexa had made after questioning Lanie's coworkers. No one had seen her disappear. No one had seen anything suspicious. No one had noticed anyone watching her or following her or threatening her.

Everything about her last night at the diner had been just as ordinary as any other night at the diner.

She'd been staring at this file for years. Maybe it was time to admit that she'd never find Lanie. Maybe it was time to accept that sometimes answers, and missing people, were never found.

Did it really matter anyway? She was sure that the only closure she was going to find or provide to her mother and grandmother was confirmation that Lanie had died, somehow, somewhere, by some mysterious hand, long ago. She didn't need to find Lanie's remains to know that.

Slamming the file shut in a show of her deep-seated

frustration, Alexa turned and held it over the trashcan next to her desk. But her fingers wouldn't release the papers to let them fall into the bin. She couldn't let go.

Swallowing hard, blinking the sheen of tears from her eyes, she spun her chair enough to shove the file back into the desk drawer and closed it hard as she stood. She couldn't stop looking. Even if she did, her mind would never rest. Holly had found a possible lead into her mother's murder twenty years later. Alexa could still find something that would help her find out what had happened to her sister.

No. She couldn't give up. What she could do was start over, with a fresh set of eyes. Once Mandy Campbell was home and safe, Alexa would spend a few days reviewing Lanie's file. She'd revisit Lanie's old coworkers and friends, gently question Mami and Abuela again. Just like Mandy's friends, maybe Lanie's friends had been feeling protective of her privacy when they'd been questioned. All these years later, perhaps one of them would be ready to tell Alexa any secrets Lanie had been keeping.

Someone knew what had happened to her sister.

Dean woke with a start. He wasn't certain what had awakened him, but Alexa was already sitting up, tuned in to the darkness. He moved to sit, but she put her hand to his chest and pushed him back down.

"Stay put," she whispered as she slipped from his bed.

He couldn't see more than shadows in shades of blue-silver cast by the waning quarter moon, but he was able to hear. The sounds of someone shuffling around in another part of the house made his heart roll in his chest and his stomach clench with anxiety.

Alexa slid her gun off the nightstand and pushed the safety off with a quiet click. Her bare feet didn't make a sound as she moved across the carpet of his bedroom. He sat up and pushed the blankets aside.

"I said to stay put," she whispered from the door.

He stopped moving. This was his house, for God's sake, but common sense reminded him that she was the one with the gun. No wise man would argue with someone holding a loaded weapon. However, when another noise sounded from the living area, he sat up taller, determined that no man would let a woman face danger alone, even if she were more qualified to do so. He stood and followed her down the hallway, despite the way she scowled up at him.

Pressing her pointer finger to her lips, she silently hushed him. Only then did he realize how heavily he was breathing. He wasn't the confrontational type, really, so the thought of a burglar snooping through the living room set him on edge more than he had initially realized. His adrenaline was flowing and his heart pounding wildly. He was panting, like he'd run a marathon instead of crept twenty feet in the darkness.

Alexa lifted her hand, another silent motion, this time a clear statement for him to stop closing in on her. He did, and she moved the last few feet of the hallway on her own before peering around the corner with her gun aimed at the floor but her finger on the trigger. She was ready to shoot should the intruder be a threat. The thought caused his stomach to roll, but then he almost laughed as he heard his mother's voice in his head.

Don't you make a mess on my carpet, young lady. That was what his mom would have said if she were there. Okay, probably not in that particular instance, but that was what popped into Dean's head. He heard her voice as clear as the bright blue sky on one of the sunny days at the lake his parents used to take them to over summer vacation. That was one of the few places where Dean didn't mind having Mandy hanging around. They would bury each other in the sand and laugh as they splashed each other to get rid of the remaining grit. Those were some of the happiest times in Dean's childhood.

The memory ended with a flash, and he crashed back to reality with Alexa's lightning-fast movement. One second she was standing there peering around the corner; the next she was standing, feet planted and gun raised, in the entry to the living room.

"Don't move," she warned in a loud, confident tone. "Put your hands up and drop to your knees."

"I-I-I live here," came a weak voice in response.

"Mandy," Dean breathed. He rushed down the hallway and flipped the switch for the overhead light. Wincing at the sudden brightness, he managed to keep his eyes open so he could confirm the twig of a girl standing in front of Alexa with her hands up and her eyes wide was his little sister.

Her makeup was mostly worn off, but mascara streaked under her eyes as if she'd been crying at some point. Despite the cooler weather, she was dressed in ripped skinny jeans, a tank top, and a flimsy pair of flip-flops.

Dean crossed the room in three long strides and pulled her into his arms. Hugging her tight, taking note of how her bones poked him back, he kissed her head as she crumbled against him. The sound of her crying brought tears to his eyes, too. She clung to him, her face buried in his chest, as her body shook with sobs muffled by his embrace.

The only other time they'd stood like that was at their mother's funeral. After the service ended and people started to drift away, Mandy refused to leave the casket. She'd stood there in her brother's arms, crying and crying, until she seemed to run out of tears. She was weak and exhausted by the time she stopped sobbing.

Tonight, she seemed weak and exhausted before she'd even begun.

Though Dean had a million questions, a thousand things to say, words wouldn't form. When she leaned back, he brushed his thumbs under her eyes, wiping some of her tears and more of her mascara away. "It's okay," he whispered. "Everything's going to be okay."

She sniffed, swallowed, and looked over his shoulder with confusion. "Who's that half-naked chick with a gun in our living room?"

He smiled and glanced over his shoulder just as Alexa was returning, now dressed in a pair of his boxers and one of his old T-shirts, carrying clothes for him as well. He accepted her offering with a whispered thanks. "Mandy, this is Alexa."

"Hi, Mandy," she said sweetly and held her hand out, but Dean could see her mind working. Silently taking in every nuance of his little sister's behavior.

Alexa was assessing the situation with an intensity he hadn't seen since they'd first met and she was sizing him and his story up. He slid his arm more tightly around Mandy's shoulders, inexplicably needing to shield her from Alexa's scrutiny.

"Are you alone?" Alexa asked, her voice still filled with the kindness that Dean had come to know, but her eyes remained shaded with suspicion.

"Yeah," Mandy said, but even Dean questioned whether the hesitantly spoken word was a lie.

"I'm just going to make sure you weren't followed." She flipped the overhead light off, and a moment later, Dean noticed her silhouette moving to the door. The lock echoed through the room as she clicked it into place. Then she went to the window and peered through the blinds.

"Who is that?" Mandy asked.

Dean hushed her as he watched Alexa looking outside. "See anything?"

"No." Turning, she hit the switch on her side of the room for the overhead light.

Alexa asked, "How did you get here, Mandy?"

Tearing her gaze from Dean to Alexa, she narrowed her eyes, clearly resenting the question. "I walked."

"From where?" Alexa pushed.

"A gas station a few miles away. Dean, who is this?"

"How did you get in?" Alexa continued.

"Who the fuck is this?" Mandy demanded of her brother.

Dean lifted his hand toward Alexa and put his other palm to Mandy's shoulder. "There's a spare key in a fake rock outside."

"That's going to change," Alexa muttered as she eased her defensive posture.

"Mandy, this is Alexa. She's a PI I hired to find you."

Mandy skimmed over Alexa's attire. "Oh, is *that* why you hired her?"

Alexa softened before Dean's eyes, changing from untrusting investigator to the sweet woman he'd so easily fallen for. "I'm sorry, Mandy. I didn't mean to come across as harsh. You startled me is all. Yes, your brother hired me to find you. He's been really worried about you." She offered that gentle smile of hers that instantly won most people over. "Obviously things have...developed...since then."

Mandy relaxed as well, but there were still questions in her glazed eyes. "So you're Dean's girlfriend?"

Alexa lifted her brows as if surprised by the realization. "Yeah. I guess I am."

"We've been looking for you everywhere," Dean said. "I'm glad you're home. Are you hungry? Thirsty?"

She nodded, not clarifying which, but it didn't matter. He'd get her both. He started for the kitchen, but Alexa put her hand on his arm before he could walk away.

"I'll get her something," she said. "You stay here."

"Maybe you should get some real clothes, too," Mandy suggested. Alexa glanced down at her bare legs.

"I'll get something more appropriate for all of us," she said lightly, as if she hadn't noticed the underlying accusation in Mandy's words.

Dean was thankful. He didn't want to let Mandy out of his sight. He wasn't sure he ever would again. Leading her to the sofa, he pulled her down and clasped her hands. "Are you okay?"

She shrugged and lowered her gaze.

"Mandy, you gotta tell me everything. I can't help if you don't tell me everything. You know that, right?"

She nodded but didn't speak.

"I'm not mad at you. I'm worried. I want to help."

"Is that why you're shacking up with a private *dick*?"

He ignored the venom in her words. She'd been through a lot, and having a woman pull a gun on her was probably the least of her traumas. "She traced the texts you sent to a phone in Chicago. We went there looking for you. We were this close to finding you when we were told you'd been moved."

Her eyes changed from the hard challenge of a border-line temper tantrum to what he could only describe as shame. Tears filled her eyes and fell unchecked. When she spoke, her voice was so soft and broken, he had to lean in to hear her. "That guy who got arrested called my handler and told him what happened. He said people were looking for me."

"That's why they were moving you?"

She bobbed her head again. "He was trading me for someone else. Like I'm a fucking football player or something."

He ran his hand over hers to try to soothe her. "How'd you get away?"

"I recognized the area when he stopped for gas. We weren't far from the mall. I made a run for it."

"You walked here all the way from the mall? Dressed like that?" Hugging her to him, trying to warm away the chill that had to have settled in her bones, Dean silently vowed to find whoever had done this to her and kill him. *Slowly.*

"Here you go," Alexa said, holding out a sweatshirt from Mandy's closet.

She then offered a T-shirt to Dean, who pulled the soft material over his head and looked up at her.

He was expecting the sweetness he'd come to know, but she was eyeing Mandy as if seeking some other truth that hadn't been spoken.

"You were going to get Mandy something to eat."

"Yeah," Alexa said as her smile returned. "Give me just a minute."

"What's her problem?" Mandy asked with an edge to her tone.

"She's just analytical. Like me. You know how I like to overthink everything."

"I don't like how she's looking at me."

He didn't either, and he didn't understand it. Alexa was hired to bring Mandy home, and here she sat. Why wasn't Alexa happier about that? Instead of being relieved, she was obviously uncertain about his sister's return.

Instead of focusing on the questions in Alexa's eyes, he put his arm around Mandy again. She was safe. She was home. That was all he had to think about at the moment. That was all he was willing to think about at the moment.

11

ALEXA JOLTED AWAKE AGAIN, only this time not to the subtle sounds of someone sneaking around Dean's house. The phone on the nightstand next to her chirped, and she grabbed it before the noise could offend her ears again.

"Yeah?" she asked, answering the call without looking at the screen.

"She's on the move," Rene said. Alexa had called her the moment she got a break from Dean to ask her to keep an eye on the house.

Alexa blinked rapidly, trying to force her brain to start working properly. Between making love to Dean and Mandy's sudden appearance, she hadn't slept but an hour or so, and her mind was clouded. "Did someone pick her up?"

"Yep," Rene answered. "I'm tailing. The plates are local, Lex."

Alexa rolled out of bed and trotted to Dean's office in

the next room. Grabbing a pen, she found a scrap of paper. "Make and model?"

Rene rattled off the information on the sedan she was following and then asked, "Did you get a tracer on her?"

"Was she wearing a gray sweatshirt when she left?"

"Yes."

"I tucked it into the hem. I'll log in and monitor once I get to the office. Be safe," Alexa said before ending the call.

"Hey," Dean mumbled from the door, his voice thick with sleep. "What's going on?"

Turning, Alexa frowned, hating that she was about to dump even more on him. He'd finally seemed relaxed, like he somehow believed everything was going to magically be okay. "She left," Alexa said, breaking the news as gently, but bluntly, as possible.

He dropped the hand that he'd been brushing through his shaggy hair. "What?" His eyes widened as his brain seemed to process what she'd said. Turning, he crossed the hall and pushed the door to Mandy's room open.

Alexa didn't have to look inside. She knew there was no one there.

Spinning on his heels, Dean rushed down the hallway, calling out to his sister.

"Dean." Alexa followed him. "Dean. She's gone."

Turning, he faced her. "Why? Why would she leave?"

Sagging under the weight of the reality she understood far more than he, she frowned. "Do you keep emergency cash in the house? Any valuables she could sell?"

Disbelief filled his eyes, but then he brushed by her to

his office and pulled a vase off a shelf. He turned it upside down, looked inside, and then rattled it for good measure. The vase was empty. Moving by her again, he went into Mandy's room and lifted the lid off the jewelry box on her dresser. Alexa knew he was looking for the diamond ring and emerald earrings that had been sitting on the crushed red velvet lining Alexa had seen when she'd searched her room soon after Dean hired her. By the way he cursed under his breath, she guessed they were gone.

He looked at Alexa with the same desperation he'd had the first time she met him. "What? She... She wasn't coming home?"

Alexa shook her head. "Honey, she's a drug addict working for a pimp who probably lost a little faith in her after his john got arrested. He needed her to prove herself to him. And in the process, they made a few bucks."

"She's going to pawn Mom's jewelry?" The hurt in his voice made Alexa's heart break.

"Rene is following her, and I put a tracer in her sweatshirt. We're going to know every move they make."

He narrowed his eyes. "You put a tracer in her sweatshirt? You knew she was going to leave? And you didn't stop her?"

She wasn't surprised by the accusation and anger in his tone, but she still felt as if he'd kicked her in the heart. "Dean—"

"You knew she was going to leave, and you didn't stop her. What the fuck, Alexa?"

"Dean. She is legally an adult. Short of kidnapping, there was nothing either of us could do to stop her."

"I could have convinced her to stay."

"Really?" She didn't mean for the sarcastic retort to leave her lips, but there it was, lingering between them. Taking a breath, she reined herself in. "She didn't come home for help. If she had, she wouldn't have left."

"That man is messing with her head."

"I know that. I do. But legally—"

"Fuck what is and isn't legal! My sister is in trouble, and she was right here. I could have helped her, but you let her go."

"We are following her."

"So what? What the hell is that going to do?"

"She stole from you, Dean. Call the police and turn her in."

"What?" He shook his head. "Are you kidding me?"

"She'll be arrested and placed in a home like the one Sandra told you about. They'll help her get sober and break the cycle her pimp has her in."

"You want me to have my sister arrested? You're insane." He pushed past her and headed toward the living room.

She followed. "Do you want to know what your other choice is?"

Dean didn't respond. He marched to the kitchen and started slamming things around as he made coffee.

Pressing her palms against the counter, she watched him. "Your other choice is to hope she comes back and if she does she's ready for help. Because she's so far gone right now, she just stole from you and is willing to pawn her dead mother's jewelry for drug money."

He still didn't respond.

"Dean. Call the police, file a report, and have her arrested before she ends up dead of an overdose or murdered by some pervert in a cheap motel room."

That got his attention. He set the coffee carafe down so hard she was surprised it didn't shatter. "Fuck you. All you had to do was tell me she was going to leave, and I could have stopped her."

"*How?* You would have locked her in her room? Tied her to a chair? Talked reason into her? Maybe you didn't notice, but that girl was stoned out of her mind sitting here. She wasn't here to get saved, Dean. She was looking for a way to get more drugs."

"Sandra said she'd take her in. She said she would give Mandy the help she needs."

"Mandy is an adult." Alexa pounded her fist against the countertop, furious that he wasn't listening and they were wasting precious time. "Until she has her rights taken away by a judge, she can sign herself out of any rehab facility you put her in. Hell, Dean, she doesn't even have to go to a rehab facility. If you have her arrested for theft, you can work out a deal to force her into getting help in lieu of going to jail." Rounding the counter, she tried to calm herself and him. "Babe, you are not understanding the gravity of this situation."

"No," he stated firmly. "You are not understanding.

My baby sister was right here, safe from that asshole who is selling her body, and you let her leave. I trusted you to help me. I literally put her life in your hands, and you let her go." He shook his head at Alexa. "Leave. Get out of my house. I don't want your help anymore."

"Dean."

He moved around her, storming away, and somewhere deep in the house a door closed with a crash. Alexa lowered her face, chewing her lip as she debated whether she should have told him her suspicions. While he'd been sitting on the couch cuddling his sister, she'd been in his room whispering into the phone. She'd called Sam and requested she reach out to the team for backup. She wanted the house watched and someone ready to follow Mandy should she make a run for it. She'd also torn the threads along the hem of Mandy's sweatshirt and hid the tracer that she always carried.

The little GPS trackers the team used were intended to find each other if necessary, but in this instance, the entire HEARTS team was going to be able to see where Mandy Campbell was...well, her sweatshirt at least. That would be enough to tell the police where to go to arrest her. If Dean would just make the call.

She used the excuse of starting a pot of coffee to give them both time to cool down. When the liquid started dripping into the carafe, she went to his room. The sound of the shower filtered through the closed bathroom door. Alexa hesitated before opening it. Steam immediately surrounded her, and she could barely make out his image through the moisture-covered glass door.

"You can be mad at me all you want," she said.

He stopped rubbing soap over his body, freezing at the sound of her voice. "I asked you to leave."

"But being mad at me isn't going to bring her home," she continued.

"And having her arrested will?"

"Yes," she stated firmly. "It will. Make the call while we can still tell the police her location. Eventually Rene will lose them and Mandy will ditch her sweatshirt. Then she'll be missing again, and you'll be back to square one."

She didn't wait for his reply. She left him to his shower and returned to his room, where she pulled his shirt off and tossed it on the bed. Dressing, she gathered her things and headed for the door. He might be too angry to do what was needed, but Alexa guessed if she and her team followed Mandy long enough, they'd find another cause to call the police on her without Dean pressing charges. Except those charges might not be dropped and the girl would have a permanent record. She might never get out from under the shadow of whoever it was that had her.

But that wasn't on Alexa. Dean had a choice to make, hard as that might be, and she couldn't make it for him. She did understand his anger. She didn't blame him. She'd had plenty of clients angry with her for making the tough calls they couldn't bring themselves to make. This one hurt, though. That was her fault for getting involved with Dean on a personal level. Rene had warned her the case could go south, as they often did, and now she was feeling the effects of that in a way she'd never felt before.

Her heart was breaking for him and for Mandy, and for herself, because she didn't want Dean to walk away from what they'd shared because of the choice she'd made and the position she was putting him in.

Fully dressed, she looked at the bathroom door. The water was still running. He was still standing there debating what he should do...or wondering why the hell he'd ever hired Alexa in the first place. Either way, she had to leave it up to him to decide the next move.

Climbing into her car, she cleared her head of the emotional turmoil and called Rene the moment she was out of Dean's driveway. "Got any updates?"

"They're headed east on the interstate. I'd guess they are going back to Chicago."

Alexa let that sink in. "That doesn't make sense. Why would he bring her all the way back here just to steal a few hundred bucks and some jewelry from her brother?"

"Testing her loyalty?"

"He's going to drive five hours one way just to test her loyalty? He could get her to mug a little old lady to do that. This isn't right, Rene."

"I agree. What are you thinking?"

"I don't know, but you can't follow them all the way to Chicago."

"I might not have to. They're exiting. I'll keep you posted."

The call ended, and Alexa heaved a sigh. She needed

to run home and grab a quick shower and change her clothes before heading into the office and tackling this day.

DEAN SAT AT THE KITCHEN COUNTER, RUNNING THE events of the night before through his mind. Not just Mandy coming home and then disappearing again but the suspicion in Alexa's eyes. The questions she'd asked. The way she'd peered through the window as if expecting to see someone watching the house...or waiting for Mandy to reemerge.

When he'd woken up, Mandy had been sneaking through the house, probably intending to never even be heard. She probably had no intention of letting him know she was home. She probably planned to sneak in, steal his cash and their mother's jewelry, and disappear without a trace. As if she'd never been there.

He'd been a goddamned fool to think that her coming home was going to be the end of this drama. Alexa had warned him, more than once, that finding Mandy was only the beginning. She was addicted to drugs. She wasn't the same little girl he remembered. She wasn't an innocent being consumed by the world. She'd been pulled into a world of drugs and prostitution and was doing whatever it took to keep going.

Including theft from her own brother. And dead mother, as Alexa had reminded him.

"Christ," he whispered as he dug his fingertip into his eyes, trying to make sense of what had transpired.

Mandy was in a world of trouble, and the one time she'd reached out for help might have been her last. That might have been the last moment of clarity she'd ever have if he didn't force his help on her. And the only way to do that, according to Alexa, was to press charges.

He heaved a breath when his phone pinged, letting him know he had received a new text message.

Alexa.

Mandy stopped at a pawnshop. Holly is on her way to get whatever she sold. Probably Lily's jewelry. I'll confirm and let you know.

He didn't know what to say to that, so he set his phone aside and stared into his coffee, which had long ago gone cold. He didn't know how long he'd been sitting there trying to determine what to do. What would his mother do? Have her own child picked up for theft? Have her face a judge who could decide to put her in jail instead of a rehab facility?

What had Alexa said? *Call the police, file a report, and have her arrested before she ends up dead of an overdose or murdered by some pervert in a cheap motel room.*

Those were the options? His only options?

Walking to the sink, he dumped out the bitter brew and turned to rest his lower back against the edge of the sink. Looking out at the living area, he scoffed at the decorations he and Alexa had put up in some pointless attempt to make Mandy's home more welcoming when she returned.

She hadn't noticed. She hadn't even realized what he'd done for her. That wasn't like his sister. Mandy loved the holidays, any holiday. She loved the decorations. She used to pester their mother weeks in advance, wanting to help her decorate and bake cookies or carve pumpkins. Whatever the season called for, Mandy used to be all in. She'd gotten that from their mother.

The reason Dean had dragged out all those damned decorations was because he remembered how disappointed she had been when he hadn't decorated for Christmas the previous year. And she hadn't noticed.

She had been stoned. Just like Alexa said. Too stoned to care about fake spiders and painted monsters and carved pumpkins. She had one thing on her mind when she'd been sitting there—getting her hands on his emergency cash and finding valuables to pawn. To buy drugs.

His sentimental sister, who refused to part with her favorite blanket no matter how ratty the material got, had just sold their deceased mother's favorite ring and earrings. To buy drugs.

She was out there selling her body, letting strange men touch her. To buy drugs.

An unexpected rush of sorrow rolled through him. Tears bit at his eyes, and his breath burst from his lungs. Holy shit. How had things gotten this bad? How had she fallen so far?

How had she gotten to the point that the only way to save her was to have her arrested?

If he did that, she might never forgive him, but if he didn't, she probably wouldn't be alive to resent his actions anyway. She was the only family he had left, and he was going to lose her. No matter what he did, he was going to lose her. But he couldn't live with himself if he didn't do everything he could to save her.

Grabbing his phone, he looked at Alexa's text before forcing his shaking fingers to type out a reply.

You're right. I need to press charges. What do I do?

She replied immediately. *I'm sending someone over.*

Dean's heart ached as he stared at her reply. Any other time she would have said she was on her way. She would have dropped whatever she was doing and run to his side. He tried not to read too much into it. She was on Mandy's trail; she was working the case. She probably couldn't stop whatever she was doing. He wasn't going to take her response personally. At least not yet.

Returning to his seat at the counter, he waited. Time seemed to slip through his hands, just like his sister's innocence had slipped through hers. Without notice. Without care.

Finally a knock at the door drew him from his thoughts. He blew out a long breath as he crossed the living room. He opened the door to find a woman he recognized from Alexa's team. Her black curly hair was pulled into a bun and her suit jacket was fitted, making her look more like a lawyer than the PI he'd seen a few times at the HEARTS office. "Tika, right?"

"Right." Her smile didn't convey the same kind of support or soothing quality that her teammate's had. "Alexa asked me to take you to the station. I've got a better understanding of the legal system than the rest of the team," she said, as if to justify why Alexa hadn't come herself. "I'll walk you through everything and answer any questions you might have. Once the police are ready to move forward, I'll get confirmation from Alexa on Mandy's whereabouts. The police will take over from there. They'll notify you once she's been arrested. You can notify Alexa, and we'll consider the case closed."

Case closed. Just like that. Mandy would be in jail. Dean would be negotiating for her to go to rehab. And then what? What would that mean for him? For his sister? For his relationship...whatever was left of it...with Alexa?

Tika's smile faltered a bit. "Dean? Have you changed your mind?"

Dean hesitated, one last moment of doubt, before stepping aside and gesturing for Tika to enter his broken home. "No. No, I haven't changed my mind."

[12]

Alexa's crummy mood didn't improve when Holly stepped through the conference room doorway. Alexa hadn't been looking forward to whatever the team leader would have to say about her crossing the line with Dean, but she definitely wasn't up for the lecture now that Dean was angry with her. She barely glanced up before returning her attention to the report she was filling out for the case that was about to close.

"How's your day?" Holly asked.

Alexa scoffed, immediately thinking of how Dean had kicked her out of his house. "Not the best. Yours?"

Holly set two coffee mugs and the bottle of vodka that had taken up permanent residence in the break-room freezer on the table across from Alexa. "This might help."

Sitting back, Alexa accepted her fate. Holly wasn't going to leave until they'd had this chat. They might as well take the edge off with a shot. Or two.

"Couldn't hurt, could it?" Alexa asked.

Reaching into her pocket, Holly pulled out a small plastic bag and slid it toward Alexa. While Alexa opened it, peering at the jewelry Mandy had pawned, Holly poured vodka into a mug.

"I know about you and Dean, Lex."

"I figured as much." She rolled the top of the bag closed and set it aside so she could take it to Dean. "There aren't any secrets in these four walls, are there?"

Holly finished pouring the second drink. "Not many, no."

"Are you pissed about it?"

Leaning across the table, Holly offered one mug before sitting across from Alexa with her own. "Pissed? No. You're a big girl. You make your own choices based on whether or not you are willing to pay the consequences. Irritated is more like it."

Alexa swallowed a sip. "Irritated?"

"Because the consequences for this particular choice impact the business, not just you. He would be well within his rights to feel that a representative of this office took advantage of him."

"I talked to him about that. I don't think that's going to be an issue."

"Well, it could be. Despite what you think. You muddied waters that are better left alone. It's done, Alexa. I'm not angry, just irritated that you would risk the reputation of HEARTS. We all work hard to diminish the stigmas attached to a group of female investigators. Having one of us sleep with a client could damage that."

Alexa lowered her gaze. "I know."

"You also knew crossing that line with Dean could lead you to this place where you are now. I am correct in thinking the cloud hanging over you today has something to do with your client's reaction to the turn his case has taken?"

Pushing aside her report, deciding now wasn't the time to worry about listing expenses, Alexa said, "He wasn't thrilled when I told him his best option was to press charges against his sister. He blamed me."

"We often get the brunt of the blame when cases don't go well. You know that."

"Yeah. I know that."

"Tell me what happened," Holly coaxed.

Alexa suspected Rene had already told her all there was to tell, and not just out of office gossip. Alexa had dragged two additional team members into her case. Someone had to explain that, and out of everyone involved, Rene was the most levelheaded. She was the one Holly would go to for answers first. Rene likely hadn't sugarcoated any of what had gone down.

"I was with Dean when his sister showed up in the middle of the night. I saw her sudden reappearance for what it was. She was there to take some things, find some money, and hit the road. Instead of calling her out on that in front of Dean, I put my tracer in her sweatshirt and called for backup. I didn't tell him what I thought...what I *knew* was going to happen. Instead I let her steal from him and run away so he'd have a legal way of forcing her to get help." She shrugged. "He thinks he could have convinced her to stay and get sober."

Holly was a master at keeping her emotions from playing across her face, but even she frowned at Dean's conviction. "He doesn't understand what he's dealing with, Lex. Either by choice or ignorance."

"By choice," she stated. "He's not a fool."

"He doesn't have to be a fool to choose to see the best in his sister. None of us want to acknowledge that our loved ones may have a dark side."

Silence fell over them, and Alexa had to wonder if Holly was thinking of her dad. Alexa would usually take the opportunity to ask and offer her support, but she was emotionally spent at the moment. She didn't have an ounce of anything left to give to someone else. She had hoped that Dean pressing charges against Mandy meant he had come to understand Alexa's motives and would reach out to her, but it had been Tika who let Alexa know the police were out looking for Mandy. The fact that she was still in the area was something that had Alexa puzzled. She just couldn't understand why Mandy had been brought back to the city where she'd been taken. That didn't make sense.

The moment of introspection passed when Holly asked, "Do you think she's gone from unwilling victim to believing these people are looking out for her?"

"I think this was a test of her loyalty to her handler."

"She passed. Now what happens to her?"

Alexa huffed a breath. "I guess she moves up the food chain. Gets a promotion, so to speak. She'll get better-quality johns, more money or drugs or whatever they are giving her as her share of payment. She'll be worth more to her handler, so she'll get treated a little better. And the better they treat her, the easier it will be for her to justify what they are putting her through. She'll get pulled deeper and deeper into this life, and we may never get her out."

She nearly choked on the last bit. The idea of not saving Mandy was unfathomable but a possibility she had to face.

"We'll get her out," Holly said. "We're not going to let them take her."

Alexa appreciated Holly's sentiment, but they both knew they might not have a choice in the matter.

"So," Holly asked. "You were together. You and Dean?"

"Yes."

"And now?"

Alexa shrugged. "I convinced him to have his sister arrested, Hol. I'm not sure there is any place to go after that."

"Someday he'll understand that you were trying to save her from herself."

She toasted her friend. "Here's to someday."

Holly laughed slightly. "I'm sorry, Lex. I suck at reassuring people. I know that. I should have sent Eva in here."

Alexa shook her head. "I don't need reassurances. I know the score. I slept with a client when he was emotionally vulnerable, and when things didn't go as planned, he blamed me. You're right. I knew the risk. I took it, and I got my comeuppance."

"You like each other, though. Even I can see that."

Finishing what was in her glass, Alexa swallowed it down to ease her heartache. "He's a good guy. A genuinely good guy. Those aren't easy to come by. In our line of work especially. As you know."

"I do know. I got lucky with Jack. Eva got lucky with Josh. Maybe once this blows over, Dean will see you did what really was best for his sister, and you'll get lucky, too. He's in a bad spot right now."

Alexa sighed. "I know that." Taking a breath, she let it out slowly, surprised at the sting she felt in her heart. "You know me, Hol. I wanted to swoop in and take all his pain away and make him better. I spend so much time trying to make everyone else better because..."

"Because fixing other people makes you feel less broken."

Alexa lifted her eyes, surprised Holly got it. Then again, she wasn't surprised at all. Not only could Holly read between the thinnest lines, but she had her own ghosts to reconcile.

Emotion slammed into Alexa's chest. "I'm never going to find Lanie, am I?" she whispered.

Holly's shoulder's sagged. "I don't know. I hope you do. I hope you find the answers you need."

"I hope we both do. Then maybe we can rest. Wouldn't that be nice? To not always be wondering what happened to them?"

A knock on the doorframe behind Holly drew Alexa's attention. Tika looked hesitant, as if she suspected she might be interrupting something.

"Hey, Tika," Alexa said.

"I just got back."

"How's Dean?"

"Quiet," Tika said. "He knew this was the right thing to do, but he wasn't happy about it. He asked about you."

Alexa sniffed and sat back. "I'll reach out to him later."

Tika's brow lifted. "Is that vodka?"

Holly held up the bottle, and Tika took it with her to the little table in the corner where a stack of cups sat next to an empty pitcher.

She poured two fingers before taking a sip. She sighed dramatically. "Hell of a day, ladies."

"Hell of a day," Alexa agreed and held out her mug for a refill.

"Are you guys day drinking?" Sam asked as she walked in. "And nobody called me?"

Tika sat next to Alexa and held up her cup. "Here's to day drinking."

Alexa toasted her. "We should probably lock the front door before a client comes in and catches us."

Sam stuck her head out of the conference room. "Eva!

Lock the front door and then come to the conference room for a drink!"

Eva squealed from her office but appeared in the conference room in what seemed like seconds. "What's the occasion?"

Alexa swished the liquid in her glass. "I had sex with my client and then suggested he have his sister arrested. I think he hates me now."

Heavy silence filled the room before Sam offered her usual sunny outlook. "Well. At least you got laid first."

It took a moment, but a laugh ripped from Alexa's chest. "Yes, I did. Multiple times." Alexa's smile faded as the moment of humor was replaced by the familiar sensation of loneliness.

"Oh, honey," Tika said, her voice filled with concern. "Don't cry. If you cry, I'll cry, and I am one seriously ugly crier. Nobody needs to see that. My face scrunches up and I get all snotty."

"I'm not going to cry," Alexa said. "I'm just... When I was little, before Lanie disappeared and everything changed, I remember the way my parents used to look at each other. My papi thought Mami hung the moon. I always said I wouldn't fall for a man who didn't look at me like that. Dean looked at me like that. But I don't know if it was real or because he thought I could save his sister. You should have seen his face when he realized I let Mandy steal from him and leave. He was so hurt. He felt completely betrayed, and I don't know if he can forgive me. Even if he does, once his sister is safe, maybe... Maybe he won't look at me the same, you know? Maybe it was never real, but just a byproduct of the pain he's going through. I was so sure that I felt something there, but maybe I'm just...so tired of being alone, I looked for something that wasn't there."

Tika put her hand on Alexa's knee, and Alexa looked up at a room full of somber faces.

Forcing a laugh, she shrugged it off. "Sorry. I don't mean to be such a downer."

"Give him time," Tika said. "Let him get through some of this mess, and then his head will clear and you'll figure out where he stands."

Alexa wrapped her fingers around Tika's hand. "And in the meantime, I have you guys. Who could ask for more?"

"Hear, hear." Holly lifted her glass.

"Oh, easy for you to say, bitch." Sam tossed the lid of the vodka bottle at Holly. "You get to go home to your *fiancé*."

The women playfully booed Holly's relationship status.

Holly rolled her eyes. "Jealousy is such an ugly emotion, ladies."

"What do you know about human emotion?" Eva asked, causing laughter to erupt through the room.

The sound soothed the ache in Alexa's heart. Until she looked at the conference room door and noticed Rene crossing the lobby. She wasn't due back to the office for two more hours, when Holly was going to relieve her from staking out the motel room Mandy and her handler had checked into. Alexa's breath caught, and she squeezed Tika's hand as her anxiety built.

"Looks like a party in here," Rene said, and the room fell silent, waiting for news. She focused on Alexa. "Mandy's been arrested. So has the man who was with her."

Alexa closed her eyes. The news, while what she'd been hoping for, was also what she'd dreaded. No doubt seeing his sister in jail would cement Dean's anger.

DEAN HAD NEVER BEEN SO EXHAUSTED IN HIS LIFE. And he'd never felt so alone.

Mandy was in jail. Her lawyer, the one Dean had hired at Tika's suggestion, was trying to convince her to agree to be released to the custody of Sandra Cawling, the social worker in Chicago. Sandra had already been notified of Mandy's arrest and was on her way to convince Mandy to spend her time in a recovery center rather than going to jail for petty theft. If she agreed, Dean would drop all charges and Mandy would be released from jail. Then Sandra would take her to an undisclosed recovery center.

He hadn't been allowed to see his sister and probably wouldn't see her until the recovery center allowed it. However, the attorney he'd hired had relayed that Mandy was furious with him. That was to be expected, he guessed. Sometimes doing the right thing for someone didn't always coincide with doing what that person wanted.

Dean scoffed at his own train of thought, his own way of justifying his actions.

Sometimes doing the right thing for someone didn't always coincide with doing what that person wanted. Like, say, setting up someone's druggie sister to get arrested and forced into treatment.

Grabbing his phone, intending to call Alexa and apologize for yet another emotional outburst, he noticed the time. Midnight. He'd be a jerk to call her in the middle of the night. An even bigger jerk than he'd already been.

Falling back onto his bed, not bothering to undress or pull the covers back, Dean rolled this long-ass day over in his mind. From waking up with Alexa to realizing what she'd done to kicking her out of his house. All the way up to walking through his front door feeling like the world had crashed down around him.

He felt hollowed out. Empty. It didn't take much to realize why. Not only was he hurting over Mandy's situation, but he was hurting over his own. Everything was happening so quickly, he had no center, no gravitational pull to keep him grounded. He hadn't spent much time with Alexa, but he'd already discovered that she was that pull, that much-needed point that he could focus on and feel like everything else would somehow fall into place.

He hoped he hadn't pissed away his chance with her. No. He refused to believe he had. Alexa was too kind, too forgiving to not understand that he'd been upset and emotional. She would forgive him and give him another chance. The issue was whether or not he deserved it. Twice now he'd gotten upset enough to kick her out of his house. That wasn't like him.

He knew that. But there was no way she could. She didn't know the calm, sensible man he usually was. She only knew the wound-up, terrified version that she'd met a week before.

Dean scoffed. A week? He'd known her a week and had already taken her to bed and allowed her to become the most calming influence he had? Shit. What the hell were they doing?

He didn't know. He couldn't make sense of it, especially when he was so physically and emotionally wiped out. All he knew was that he was terrified of blowing their brief but intense relationship.

Resting his arm over his eyes, he tried to get his brain to slow down enough for sleep to find him. Instead he replayed memories of Alexa smiling, putting her gentle hand to his arm, straddling his hips…

"Damn it." Sitting up, he grabbed his phone. He wouldn't call her at this hour, but if he didn't do something, he was never going to rest.

Opening their last text conversation, he stared at her message letting him know she'd send someone over to help him press charges against Mandy. Running his fingers over the touchscreen, he sent her another message.

I'm sorry for lashing out. May I stop by the office to see you?

He set his phone down, not expecting a response until morning, but his phone beeped almost immediately.

Please do, Alexa said.

Dean smiled. *Why are you still up?*

Worrying about you.

Relief filled the void in his chest. If she were worrying about him, she probably already had forgiven him. Even so, he typed out, *I'm so sorry. I was upset.*

I know. It's okay.

No, it's not.

Hungry? she asked.

Dean laughed. Actually laughed. *Lonely.*

You should invite me over.

At midnight?

I don't have a curfew. Do you? she asked, and he swore he heard the mischief in her voice.

Come over, he replied.

On my way.

His heart already felt ten pounds lighter. She didn't hate him. She wasn't mad at him. Just like he'd figured. But he was frustrated with himself. He had to do better with her. She deserved better. If it weren't for Alexa, he never would have found Mandy. He never would have realized how much he needed someone like Alexa in his life. He'd never considered himself the needy type, but he needed her. Like he needed his next breath.

Dragging his hand over his weary eyes, he noticed how

scruffy his face was. He had taken Alexa's request that he not shave to heart, but he was closing in on a full beard and mustache. And he smelled, he realized, like stale body odor from the nervous sweat that had covered him as he'd filled out the paperwork to have his sister taken into custody.

Jumping up, he tore his clothes off as he rushed toward the shower. The water was still cold when he stepped in. He couldn't do anything about the hair covering his face, but he could rinse the stink from his skin so Alexa didn't have to smell him.

He lathered his body wash over his chest and under his arms before rinsing. He quickly dried and pulled a clean pair of house pants and a T-shirt on and then ruffled his hair with a towel to rid it of some of the dampness. He was filling two glasses with wine when he heard a car door in his driveway. Forget being ten pounds lighter; his heart started to freaking dance. He rushed to meet her, desperate to hold her in his arms, have her scent surround him, as he promised to be a better man going forward.

Jerking the door open, he was met instead with someone tackling him. A shoulder shoved hard against his chest, and Dean flew back into the entryway, stumbling until his lower back rammed into the small table where he dropped his keys. The corner jammed into him, taking his breath away. Wrapping his arm around the head, he put a chokehold on whoever was assaulting him as he attempted to fight back. A punch landed against Dean's other side, taking what was left from his lungs.

"Asshole," the man grunted. "You fucking asshole."

Only then did Dean recognize the voice. "David," he gasped out. Grabbing at his stepbrother's shirt, he shoved him back, grasping his arms to stop David from hitting him again. "Stop."

His plea was futile. David struck out, hitting Dean in the chin. He immediately tasted his own blood as his front teeth cut into his bottom lip. Before he could react, David cried out and dropped to his knees.

Dean met Alexa's confused eyes. She focused on the blood gushing from his mouth, and anger filled her face. She bent David's arm farther, and he cried out. Then he was on his stomach and she was reaching for her gun.

"No!" Dean lifted his hands. "This is David. My stepbrother."

Alexa looked up at Dean but didn't ease her hold. "What is going on here?"

"You had her arrested!" David screamed.

"Let him up." Dean dragged his palm across his mouth, looked at the blood, and then wiped his hand down his thigh as Alexa lifted David but didn't fully release him.

"Settle down, or I'll break your wrist," she warned.

David stopped fighting, but when he looked at Dean, his eyes were narrowed and his jaw set. "You had your own sister arrested."

"My sister needs help."

"You think she's going to get it in jail?"

"She's not going to stay in jail, David. As soon as she

agrees to rehab, I'll drop the charges. Her attorney is working out a deal."

David jerked toward him, but Alexa twisted her hold and he stopped. "You're going to send her to rehab over a little pot?"

"A little pot..." Dean drew a long breath and slowly lifted his gaze to Alexa. "D."

"For David," she said. "You were supplying Mandy with drugs?"

"Marijuana," he stated. "And this asswipe had her arrested for it."

Dean closed the distance and menace found his voice. "And what were you demanding in exchange for giving my sister pot?"

David's anger shifted to confusion. "What?"

"In her journal," he said coolly, "she implied that if she wanted more pot, she'd have to sleep with her dealer. D." Grabbing David's shirt, Dean pulled him nose to nose. "Were you forcing her to have sex with you in exchange for drugs?"

"No. Man, she's my sister, too. What the hell?"

"*Stepsister*." Dean jerked him closer. "What was she giving you?"

"She was getting your dad off my ass, okay?" David jerked back, and Dean eased his hold. "As soon as he found out I'd sold you pot, he wouldn't back off. He was going through my shit, threatening to kick me out."

"Well, you are, what, twenty-two now? Old enough to be on your own."

"And I would be if he didn't keep tossing my stash. I knew Mandy was smoking. We worked out a deal. I'd supply her, and she'd distract your old man long enough for me to sell and save up some money. I was going to find a place. She was going to move in with me after gradua-tion. We were going to be there for each other. Like our parents never were. Like you and Maggie never were."

"I was there for my sister."

"Were you? Really?"

Dean ground his teeth. "Do you know what's been happening to her?"

"Your dad said she ran away. Because of you."

"She's been..."

Alexa moved to Dean's side and eyed David. "Dean hired me to find Mandy. I did."

"Where?"

Dean swallowed hard before answering. "Being prosti-tuted in Chicago."

The air left the room, and the color drained from David's face. He looked to Alexa, as if he thought Dean had lied.

"She came home last night and stole from me," Dean continued. "I had her arrested so she could get help to get sober and escape the man who has been selling her."

"Mandy wouldn't..." David's wide eyes danced from one to the other. "She wouldn't."

Alexa frowned at his denial. She'd likely grown tired of how everyone seemed to have their heads in the sand over what Mandy would or wouldn't do. "She got pulled into a situation that got out of her control and led her to being sold and taking drugs. She's not herself right now. Dean did what was necessary to break the cycle before it consumed her."

"I don't believe you," David said, but his tone contradicted his words. "She's too smart for that. She's got plans. A future."

"That she pissed away by getting addicted to drugs. Drugs *you* provided her." Dean exhaled slowly so he didn't choke his stepbrother. "It was more than marijuana, wasn't it? What else were you giving her?"

He lowered his gaze.

"What else was Mandy taking?" Alexa pressed.

Dean's rage returned, but before he could beat an answer out of David, he looked up.

"We went out one night. Partying and drinking. Mandy was acting crazy, hyped up like I'd never seen her before. I asked her what she was on, just joking around, but she told me someone had given her crystal meth."

Dean's chest clenched. "What?" he asked, the word whispered in shock.

"I told her how stupid that was, Dean," David was quick to insist. "I told her. The next day when we sobered up, I sat her down and made her promise not to do that again. She swore she wouldn't."

"She might not have had a choice," Alexa said quietly. "Meth is highly addictive. One time can get someone hooked."

"I told her that," David said quietly. "She promised she wouldn't do it again."

"She's in trouble," Dean said. "I had no other way to get her into rehab. Do you really think I want to see my little sister in jail?"

"Your dad said..."

"My dad is an ass. You know that as well as I do."

David nodded once. "What's next? For Mandy?"

"If she'll agree, she'll go to rehab someplace where no one, including the men who hurt her, can find her. Once they deem her sober, they'll work on helping her cope with the trauma of what she's been through. They'll send her home when she's ready."

David's shoulders sagged. "Holy shit."

"Yeah," Dean agreed.

Looking up, David focused on Dean's lip. "I'm sorry, man. Mom said Mandy had called your dad, crying, begging for help because you'd had her arrested. Dad went to the jail, but they wouldn't let him see her."

"They won't until she's been fully processed," Alexa offered. "But if she takes the deal Dean has offered, that won't happen."

"She hasn't accepted?"

"Not that I've heard."

"Why wouldn't she?"

"Because part of the deal is her testifying against the man who was selling her. I want that bastard to pay for what he did."

"Think of it as brainwashing," Alexa offered. "Or

Stockholm syndrome. She's protecting the man who she thinks has been taking care of her. He manipulates his victims into loyalty. She doesn't know what she's doing."

"There is a social worker who is going to meet with her," Dean explained. "She's been through this type of situation before. She's going to help Mandy get through this. I trust her."

David nodded. "Okay. I...I'm sorry. I thought you were just being an ass. Your dad twisted things around."

"Dad doesn't believe Mandy's in trouble. He refuses to hear the truth."

Smirking, David said, "That's *so* unlike him. Will you keep me posted? On how things are going with Mandy? She's my sister, too. And you're my brother. Even if we are the most fucked-up family ever blended."

Dean offered him a weak smile, not really buying that last bit. David had never looked at Dean like family. He guessed the only reason he had bonded with Mandy was drugs and dissing the rest of their family. Even so, it was nice to have someone seem to be on his side for once.

"I'm sorry," David said. "About busting in here."

"Forget it," Dean offered. "I understand. I'll call you."

"Thanks. And"—he looked at Alexa—"thank you for finding her."

Alexa didn't respond as they watched David leave. Only once the door closed did Dean finally turn to face her. Putting his hand to her cheek, he was going to kiss her, but she dipped her head and peered at his mouth.

"You need ice on that lip."

"Wait." He stopped her before she could leave him. Instead of kissing her like he wanted, he rested his forehead to hers. "I've been an emotional train wreck the last few weeks. I've lashed out at you twice now. I'm usually calmer than that. I don't mean to take it out on you. I'd never mean to take it out on you. I'll do better. That's what I wanted you to come here for. To promise that I'll do better."

Resting her hands on his hips, she leaned back. "Look at me," she whispered. "Look into my eyes."

He did. He stared into her beautiful, dark, analytical gaze. She stared back. He didn't know what she was seeking, but she seemed to have found it. She gave him that sweet, comforting smile he'd grown to love, and she brushed her nose against his as she stroked his cheek.

"Let's ice your lip," she whispered, "or I'll never get what I came here for."

Dean smiled, finally feeling like the mess that had become his life was starting to sort itself out.

Alexa slid a pancake onto Dean's plate as he sipped coffee and pressed his phone to his ear. Sandra Cawling had called before heading to the police station to visit with Mandy. Alexa couldn't hear her side of the conversation, but the scowl on Dean's face let her know the conversation wasn't what he wanted to hear.

"Listen," he said, "the most important thing is getting her to agree to rehab. If she continues to refuse to testify, take that off the table. We can approach it with her later."

Alexa agreed with his suggestion and hoped Sandra did as well. Getting Mandy off drugs and out of the reach of her extortionist was the most pressing issue. The scumbag who had done this to her would get what was coming to him. Alexa had already decided that, and she had no doubt she'd have the HEARTS on her side. They'd get the evidence needed to send him to jail, with or without Mandy. Although having her cooperation would make life so much easier.

"Thanks, Sandra," Dean said before ending the call.

"Well?" Alexa pressed when he groaned miserably.

He dragged a hand over his face as he did when he was processing bad news and blew out his breath. "Well, my sister is being her usual stubborn self. She won't give up the name of the guys who did this to her. She insists she wasn't being sold. She won't cop to anything. Oh, except stealing from me, but she insists she did that all on her own and the guy who was waiting for her outside knew nothing about it. They let him go." He tossed his phone down, and Alexa immediately took his hand.

"Hey. Calm down. He's not getting away with anything. I'll find him."

Dean pressed his lips together. "I hired you to find my sister. You've done that."

"This isn't about saving Mandy now. This is about saving every other vulnerable woman who crosses his path. You really think I'm going to leave a predator out there when I can stop him?"

Pulling her hand to his mouth, he kissed her knuckles and sighed. "You really think you can find him?"

Narrowing her eyes, she playfully asked, "Do you really think I can't?"

Smiling, he shook his head. "I have complete faith in you."

Returning his grin, she asked, "Do you think Mandy will talk to you?"

"I doubt it."

"Would she talk to David? I need to know how he found her last night. Then I'll follow her steps backward until I find the man who had her at the gas station."

"Sounds like she and David had gotten close. She might."

"Would you call him? Ask him to try."

He looked at his watch. "I will. After we eat and take a shower. I want to spend some time with you before this consumes me again."

She smiled and ran her fingers over his beard. "You know, when I said you should never shave again, I was being facetious."

He covered her hand, pressing her palm against his hairy cheek. "I have considered trimming. But I won't shave. I know what pleases my woman."

Though his tone was teasing, his words wrapped around her heart and settled there. His woman? She liked the sound of that. A lot. "That's a good thing to know," she whispered. "How's your lip this morning?"

He deliberately ran his tongue over the bruised flesh. "Functional."

"Functional is all I need." Rounding the counter, she slid her arms around his neck. "Sleeping next to you was wonderful, but you know that's not why I came running over here at midnight, right?"

"No?"

She shook her head.

"Was it to save me from getting my ass kicked?"

Chuckling, she shook her head again.

He rested his hands on her hips and pulled her body against his. "So why'd you come running?"

Closing the distance even more, she pressed her cheek to his, sighing with the instant pleasure that rolled through her, not just at his nearness but at the prick of his facial hair against her sensitive skin. A quivering breath left her lips. "Tell me more about pleasing your woman."

"Oh, fuck," he said under his breath, making her smile.

He slid his hands up her thighs, under the T-shirt she'd borrowed, and tugged her panties over her hips until they fell down her legs, crumpling at her feet. Alexa stepped out of the lacy material as he lifted the hem of her shirt. And just like that, she was naked before him and his mouth was latched to her nipple. Digging her fingers in his hair, she rolled her head back and said his name on a sigh.

He slid his hand between her legs, pressed his fingers deep inside her, and then kissed his way up her neck. "This is how I want to start every day," he whispered in her ear before nipping at the lobe. "You naked and ready for me."

Alexa grinned. "I'll see what I can do."

Standing, Dean kissed her lips firmly. "I'm going to grab a condom. You bend over that barstool and wait for me."

"Say please."

He cupped her ass, squeezing as he pulled her against his erection. "Please. I'm begging you."

"In that case..." She leaned forward, resting her elbows

on the padded seat, and looked over her shoulder. "Like this."

Dean took in the scene she'd created and heaved a sigh. "I may never let you move again."

Alexa widened her smile. "That sounds promising."

He ran his fingers down her spine. "Stay."

She spread her legs farther and bent over more, giving him better access to her body. She listened to his rushed footsteps headed toward the bedroom, the drawer of the nightstand opening, and his hurried return. Her heart pounded with anticipation as he crossed the room to her. Closing her eyes, she gripped the edge of the barstool. She'd told him the first time they'd made love that she wasn't the submissive type. She'd been wrong. She hadn't been the submissive type. For him, she thought she'd do just about anything.

Biting her lip as he slid deep inside her, she laughed at how easily her convictions changed where Dean was concerned, because, in that moment, she *knew* she'd do anything for this man.

That feeling, and the sensation of him making love to her, kept her spirits sky-high as she showered and readied for work. She would prefer to stay in his bed all day, but she had reports to write to wrap up Mandy's case and officially stop working for her lover. She also wanted to talk to HEARTS about taking some time to find the bastards behind the trafficking ring that had lured Mandy in. She'd do it on her own time if needed, but she suspected her team would be more than happy to help out.

"You look amazing," Dean said as Alexa leaned close to the bathroom mirror, dabbing at her lipstick.

She couldn't stop the smile that spread across her face. "Keep up the sweet talk, Mr. Campbell, and I'll have to get naked again."

"Don't make promises you don't intend to keep." He crossed the room and nuzzled her neck. "I reached out to David. I'll let you know what I hear from him."

Turning, she put her hands to his face. "Everything's going to be okay, Dean. Even if Mandy doesn't turn in the men who did this. She's safe now. She's going to get help. Focus on that."

"I am. And on you. And us. Only good things from now on."

Giving him a quick kiss, she pressed her head to his. "I don't want to leave, but I have to get to the office before the morning meeting. Our afternoon meeting wasn't very productive, so we have a lot to catch up on this morning."

She smiled, thinking of the previous afternoon. Though she'd been heartbroken thinking her relationship with Dean might end before it really began, she'd loved sitting around the table drinking on the clock with her team. They'd never done that before, but she thought maybe it wasn't such a bad thing to suggest again someday. The women didn't spend as much time bonding like that now that Holly was engaged and Eva and Josh had gotten back together. She really hoped she could add herself to the list of teammates who would be too busy spending time with a significant other to commit to drinking with the ladies. She loved her team, but being like this with Dean was everything she'd been missing.

Stepping into his arms, she hugged him as tightly as she could. "I'll check in with you later."

Dean kissed her head. "Have a good day."

Leaning back, she smiled up at him, and her heart filled when he looked down at her in the way that made her heart sing. The way she'd always wanted someone to look at her. She bit her tongue before she said something silly and foolish and scared him away. She had a tendency to do that—jump the gun and say something committal that made men run for the hills. She wasn't going to sabotage this relationship. Not this one. Not this time.

So she pulled away from him and gathered her things before heading for the door.

"Hey," she called before stepping outside. She held his gaze as he shoved his hands in his pants pockets. "There's no telling how many unsavory people know that Mandy's house has a key hidden just outside the door. Change the lock. Today. Please?"

"Will do."

"Thank you."

"Lex?"

She looked back, taking in how absolutely adorable he looked standing there. His hair was still damp from their shower and poking out in a million directions, his beard was filling in, and when he smiled, his eyes filled with that warmth that won her over every time.

"Tell Abuela I'm taking care of your dinner tonight. Pretty sure it's my turn to feed you for a change."

Her cheeks hurt from how wide her smile had spread. "I'll let her down gently. Change this lock," she said on her way out.

She didn't stop smiling all the way to the office, and when she walked in, Sam glanced up and squealed.

"Oh. Em. Gee. You guys made up."

Alexa laughed but didn't answer as she headed straight for the conference room. "I'm late. I know. I'm sorry."

"Morning sex?" Eva asked. "Because that's why I was late."

"Just rub it in," Tika muttered.

Dropping into the seat she always took at the conference table, Alexa tried to wipe the blatant happiness off her face. "We really don't need to picture you and Josh getting it on. The dude is like a brother to us. Keep that to yourself."

"So you don't want to know how he—"

"No!" Alexa screamed.

Eva laughed but simmered down as Holly and Rene walked into the room. Now that everyone was there, the meeting would get started.

"May I start today?" Alexa asked.

"Go for it," Holly told her.

"You all know Mandy has been arrested. She isn't talking about the men who did this to her, but Dean is willing to let that part of the deal go if she keeps pushing back. He really just wants her in rehab. Her stepbrother confessed to being her pot dealer, but someone else supplied her with meth, which was probably what led to her downward spiral. Since we were hired to find Mandy and we have, this case is closed. However..." She let the word hover. "I want to find the bastards who did this to her. It's not like any of us are surprised that there are human trafficking rings operating in our city, but I feel obligated to shine a light on this particular one. I want permission, and maybe a little help, bringing these fuckers down."

Holly nodded her agreement. "I think we all want this stopped. Feel free to use our resources. I'll help any way I can."

"This could be the first step." Rene opened the manila file she'd carried into the room. "We were all a bit too distracted yesterday to worry about this, but here are a few pictures of the guy who was waiting for her outside Dean's house as well as his car and license plate. The car is registered to—"

Alexa gawked at the photo as her stomach tightened. "Are you fucking kidding me?"

"I'm guessing you recognize him?" Rene asked.

She tossed the picture down and nodded her head. "I gotta talk to Dean. This isn't over yet."

DEAN OPENED THE DOOR, AND A SMILE BROKE ACROSS

his face when he found Alexa standing there. However, his happiness faded like the sun on a cloudy when she pulled her tortoiseshell sunglasses off and met his eyes.

"Oh, shit," he muttered. "What now?"

She held up a folder. "Rene snapped a few pictures of the guy who picked up Mandy after she left the other night."

"Her handler?"

"Well, we assumed it was her handler, but maybe he was just...someone she trusted."

She stepped in, and he put his hand low against her stomach to stop her from bypassing him.

"Kiss me hello before ruining my day."

She pressed her lips to his, and he soaked up the moment, convinced the drama he thought had ended was about to continue. She dropped onto the sofa and patted the seat next to her.

"Can we just run away?" he asked, only half kidding. "Right now. Let's just pack our bags and go."

She drew a breath. "You have no idea how much I wish we could. But if we don't get to the bottom of this new information, Mandy may walk out of rehab and right back into the mess we're trying to save her from."

Dean sat and planted his elbows onto his knees as he dragged his fingers over his eyes and moaned with frustration. "Is this nightmare ever going to end?"

"It will." She ran her hand over his back, but for the first time, that didn't seem to ease his stress.

"Let me have it. Whatever it is."

She opened the file and handed him a photo. His heart dropped to his stomach as he closed his eyes and sighed. The image was grainy from having been blown up, but the face was undeniably his stepbrother. David had been waiting in the car outside his house while Mandy had lied and manipulated and stolen.

David had been the man arrested alongside Mandy, the man she had refused to identify. The man who, presumably, had been the handler overseeing her as she'd been sold online to strange men.

Stay calm, he told himself. *Breathe and stay calm.* "He was here. Last night. Blaming *me* for what she was going through."

"We don't know the full situation. She may have reached out to him when she got back to town. She may have told him she just needed to stop by and get a few things. He may not have known."

Dean ran his hand through his hair. "Do you believe that?"

"I'd like to confront Mandy, if it's okay with you," Alexa said instead of answering him. "I think it's better to try to get information from her. I don't think you should let David know about this."

"He was fishing for information, wasn't he? Trying to find out what I know."

"I don't know, Dean. But I think the best way to find out is to corner Mandy and make her think he's turned on her. I'll get what I can from her, and then *I* will take this to David and see if I can play them against each other. If there's anything to play, that is. He really might not have known."

"I don't know how much longer I can go through this," he whispered as a sense of defeat rolled over him. It was him against his entire family, it seemed. Even the person he was trying to save didn't want him involved. He was losing steam. His determination was fading.

Alexa wrapped her hands around his arm and rested her chin on his shoulder. "I can stop giving you updates if you want. I can keep this all to myself unless I absolutely have to bring something to you."

He let her suggestion sink in. "I might take you up on that. It's getting to be a bit too much. I thought we were nearing the end."

"I'm sorry."

Covering her hand, he sat back. "What if Mandy won't see you?"

"I'm going to talk through this with Sandra. She'll have better insight on how to get through to your sister. Do me a favor. Stay away from your family—all of them—but most especially David. I need to find out what is going on without us tipping them off."

"This is so fucked up."

Resting her head on his shoulder, she entwined her fingers through his. They sat like that, not speaking, as he soaked in the latest bit of information she'd uncovered. Finally she sat up and kissed his cheek.

"I need to go," she whispered. "Are you okay?"

"I will be."

"What time should I be here for dinner?"

He had to think about her question before remembering he'd promised to take care of her tonight. "Uh, let's plan to eat at six."

"Want me to bring anything? Need more candy for the trick-or-treaters?"

Hugging her against him, he kissed her head. "No. I just need you," he whispered, honestly wishing they could run away, at least for a while.

She stood, but he held her hand, not letting her leave.

"Remind me that I'm in the right, here," he said.

Leaning down, she cupped his face and kissed him firmly on the lips. "You are very much in the right. You're saving her. You're the only one saving her. Your mom would be so proud of how you're taking care of your sister. Don't forget that."

She left, and he sat there, miserable and feeling all alone.

Grabbing a photo of his mother, he brushed his thumb over her smiling face. "I hope she's right, Mom. Because I'm starting to think it's better to just let Mandy hit bottom and find her own way out."

Setting the picture aside, he sank deeper into the sofa, wishing he had one...just *one*...family member on his side.

[14]

ALEXA WASN'T INTIMIDATED by Mandy's nasty glare. The girl looked more like she was on the verge of a temper tantrum than any kind of violent outburst. The jumpsuit that had replaced her torn jeans and sweatshirt nearly swallowed her, leaving just her pale face and dark, finally brushed, hair sticking out. The short sleeves exposed her arms, and Alexa noticed fading track marks she hadn't seen when the girl had shown up at Dean's unannounced. She wasn't surprised by the signs of drug use or that she had missed the light bruises. She'd been more focused on Mandy's body language and trying to get a clear idea of why she'd returned out of the blue.

She was sorry for Dean that she had guessed right that Mandy had returned for cash to get her next fix. But she was glad that her instinct had led to Mandy's arrest and her subsequently getting the help she so clearly needed.

Sitting back, patiently waiting her out, Alexa considered how Dean was much better off letting her handle this. Seeing his sister rage like this probably would have torn what was left of his heart out.

"I'm not talking to you," Mandy said between gritted teeth. "You might as well leave."

"Mandy," her attorney soothed. "You will benefit greatly from any cooperation you offer."

"I don't have to."

"That's why it's called cooperation," Alexa offered.

Rolling her eyes, Mandy looked around the cinder-block room that echoed their words around them. She kept her hands clasped and her jaw clenched.

"I know David is your drug dealer," Alexa said, pushing the button she suspected would set the girl off.

Mandy's eyes widened, something like glazed concern filling them.

"Is he also the one who sent you to motel rooms to meet men?"

The concern faded to a blatant fuck-you look. "Don't be stupid."

Alexa shrugged. "If he isn't above getting you addicted to drugs, why should I think he's above selling your body?"

"David didn't get me addicted to drugs. He helped me when nobody else would. Dean's so fucking full of himself."

"Dean is the only one looking out for you."

Mandy sank back in the hard chair. "Is that why I'm locked up?"

"Yes," Alexa stated firmly. "Because if you weren't

here, Mandy, you'd be looking for your next high. You'd be thinking that the best way to make a quick buck is to have sex with a stranger for cash. You'd be thinking that maybe things weren't so bad in Chicago."

Mandy's scowl deepened.

"Am I wrong?"

"What's Darrin's last name?" Alexa asked, still assuming the man Mandy's roommate thought was an abusive boyfriend was actually a handler.

Mandy met her gaze but didn't open her mouth.

"Help me find him," Alexa said softly. "Help me stop him before he hurts anyone else."

"He'd kill you."

"I appreciate your concern, but I can take care of myself." Alexa leaned forward on the cold table between them. "Mandy, everyone is looking at David right now. Everyone is blaming him. Help me prove that he didn't do this to you."

"He didn't. He was just helping me."

"Tell me how he helped you."

Swallowing, she glanced at her attorney before focusing on her hands. "When Mom got sick... It was too much. I couldn't take seeing her like that. The medicine that was supposed to make her better just kept making her more and more sick. David came over one night. I thought that was crazy. We were never close to him. He and Maggie were our replacements. Dad's perfect new family. So I...I eavesdropped as he sold Dean some pot. Despite what Dean thinks, I was never Mom's little princess. I'd smoked pot before. I got ahold of David and told him what I saw, told him I wanted my own stash. We started talking after that. We'd get stoned and got closer. He never sold me pot. He shared his, so you got nothing on him. He's not a dealer."

"Your journal says—"

Mandy sat forward, her eyes wide. "You read my fucking journal?"

"Maybe you don't understand what you've put Dean through—"

"Fuck Dean." She smirked. "But I guess you already have."

"Several times," Alexa said dismissively, refusing to be baited by the girl.

"So go crawl back into his bed and leave me alone."

"I could." Alexa shrugged. "He hired me to find you, and here you are. My job is done."

"Then why are you here?"

"My sister is missing, too. She disappeared twelve years ago and hasn't been seen since."

Some of Mandy's defensive posture eased.

"I know the fear your brother was feeling, Mandy, because I've felt it, too. Not knowing where you were or what was happening to you was killing him slowly. I know that because I've felt it. I still feel it. Every single day. My sister is probably dead. She probably has been dead for a long time, but I don't know that. And I don't know how she died or why or if she suffered. You might not believe it, you might not care, but Dean was terrified for you. *For* you. He suffered because he was scared that you were suffering. He came to my office, and he begged me to believe that you were in trouble and to help him because no one else would. Not the police, not your father, not even David. It was Dean who sensed you were in trouble and moved heaven and earth to find you. No one else."

Mandy's shoulders were in a full slump by the time Alexa finished lecturing her.

"He always was pushy," she muttered, but some of the edge in her tone had abated.

Feeling like maybe she'd made some leeway, Alexa softened her tone. "According to your journal, *D* was giving you drugs in exchange for something. So here's what I'm thinking. David was providing you with pot and you guys were forming your sibling bond and all that, but *D...Darrin* was selling you something else. When your money ran out, he offered you an alternative way to get the drugs you'd become addicted to. Before you even realized what was happening, he was treating you like a piece of meat instead of a human being, and in exchange for supplying you with drugs, Darrin sent you around to Chicago's sleaziest motels. Am I right?"

The way Mandy's lip trembled and her pale cheeks flushed, Alexa suspected she had nailed the story down perfectly.

"He used you, Mandy," she said, losing the confrontational tone that had gotten the girl's attention. "He got you hooked on drugs knowing he could manipulate you and turn you into something you never wanted to be so he could make money off selling you. You aren't the first girl he's done this to, are you? There are others. You reached out to Dean, you texted him and asked for help, because you know this isn't the life you want or deserve."

Something that looked like guilt filled Mandy's eyes just before she lowered her face.

"You said you ran away from your handler. Was that true?"

The girl nodded but didn't look up.

"You ran away and came home."

Defiance had filled her eyes when she lifted her head. "Because I knew where Dean kept his cash. I hit the road the first chance I got, didn't I?"

"Yeah, you did. But I think part of you reached out to Dean and went home to Dean because you knew he'd find a way to help you. You knew he was the one who would step in and help you. David isn't going to help you, Mandy. He's going to give you drugs and listen to you gripe about how hard your life is and how unfairly Dean treats you, but he isn't going to help you."

"Dean isn't my father. He's my brother. He never acted like that. He always just tried to—"

"Push you to do better. To be better. Maybe he wasn't perfect, maybe he was too hard on you, but that's because he loves you. He hired me because he has been scared to death about what has been happening to you. He's the only one who has been looking for you, Mandy. Everyone else wrote you off. Dean is the only one who didn't give up on you."

"He had me arrested."

"Because this was the last chance he had to get you help. And you are going to get help. Whether you get sober sitting in a cold jail for the next few months or sitting in a comfortable rehab center is up to you, but you will get sober. The rehab center is nicer, kinder, and will give you a better chance at continued sobriety. A jail cell will keep you confined long enough to get the drugs out of your system. Dean isn't punishing you. Someday you'll see that and understand that this isn't how he wanted things to go. But this is where we are. This is where you are. And you are in a position to help me stop Darrin from destroying other young women the way he has destroyed you. I just need his last name."

Mandy looked at the plain wall again, but her mind was clearly trying to work through the scenario Alexa had laid before her.

"You can get out of here today, Mandy. Tell me Darrin's last name and agree to get treatment, and you'll be in a car on the way to a rehab center tonight."

"He uses several names. You won't find him by running his name through some database."

"So how do I find him?"

Mandy pondered for several seconds before looking at Alexa again. When she did, her eyes were filled with tears. "He'll be on social media. Use the hashtag *d4dank*. All one word, the number four. He'll answer."

"Which platform?"

"Any. He's very industrious." Frowning, she picked at

a broken nail for a few seconds before meeting Alexa's gaze. "The lady from the rehab center said I won't be allowed contact with anyone for a few months."

"That's right. It's best if you cut ties for a while so you can focus on getting clean."

"So I guess...I won't see Dean for a while, then?"

Alexa shook her head, not certain why Mandy was asking.

"Tell him...tell him I didn't mean for this to happen." She blinked rapidly, but the tears in her eyes fell. "It's not his fault I messed up."

"I'll tell him."

"Hey," Mandy called as Alexa stood. "This is bigger than Darrin. You know that, right?"

"I know."

"Taking him down isn't going to change anything."

Holding her gaze, she offered Mandy a soft smile. "That's not true, honey. It will change *everything* for the girls he was planning to traffic. I'll see you when you get out of rehab."

DEAN DID HIS BEST TO KEEP HIS MIND OFF HIS troubles, but they seemed to be all-consuming. As soon as he could stop dwelling on having his sister arrested, he started thinking about the role his stepbrother had in her downward spiral. Dean was slightly relieved now that Mandy had confirmed to Alexa that Darrin was the man

STOLEN HEARTS / 239

who pulled her into the sex ring, but Dean couldn't help but think David unintentionally encouraged her down the path to taking harsher drugs. No matter what he did, he couldn't stop dreading the next layer in this family drama.

However, all that faded to black when someone knocked on the door and he glanced at his watch. Rubbing his hands together, he glanced at the dining room table on his way to the door. Two place settings, a bottle of wine, and candles just waiting to be lit. Perfect.

Pulling the door open, he froze upon seeing Alexa dressed up for Halloween. She had drawn an exaggerated widow's peak on her forehead. A tight black dress showed off a more than ample amount of her full cleavage. "You are the sexiest damn vampiress the world has ever seen."

She muttered a response he couldn't understand before she spit a set of vampire teeth into her palm. "We've got candy to hand out in"—she checked her watch—"ninety minutes. Where is your costume?"

He looked down at his jeans and Def Leppard T-shirt. Stepping aside, he gestured for her to enter. "In the closet. Unlike you, I can be ready in five minutes."

"Oh." She playfully swatted his arm as she leaned up and kissed him. "You look tired."

"You look amazing."

"Yeah? Maybe if you're good, I'll wear this well after trick-or-treating is over."

Sliding his arm around her back, he pulled her against him. "I've always wanted to have sex with the undead."

She drew a breath as if to speak but then tilted her

nose up. "Whatever you are cooking smells peppery and delicious."

"It is peppery and delicious. And just about ready. Drop your bags on the couch and I'll serve."

He looked over his shoulder when she squealed with excitement. Peering at the bowl full of little faces he'd drawn on the candy-filled plastic eggs, she set her briefcase and overnight bag down and then snagged an egg and laughed.

"These are fantastic, Dean. Your mom would love that you did this."

"I think so, too." He actually had enjoyed drawing faces on the eggs and slipping treats inside, knowing the kids who came to the door would think what he'd done was fun. He'd never cared before, but he thought he might be starting to understand why his mom and sister had always gotten so excited for the holidays. Participating in something other than getting his friends together to toilet-paper each other's houses like he'd done when he was younger was pretty cool. Hearing Alexa's little laughs of approval wasn't so bad either.

Dean didn't want to ask, didn't want to cloud this feeling of happiness he'd found, but he couldn't stop himself. "How did it go with Mandy?" he pressed as he checked the dinner he'd been cooking.

Dropping a plastic egg back into the bowl, his little vampiress crossed the room and leaned on the counter. "She gave me the information I need to find Darrin. And she agreed to rehab."

His heart swelled. "She did?"

"And she asked me to tell you that none of this is your fault. Things just got out of her control."

"She's not angry at me?"

"Well," she sighed, "I wouldn't go that far, but I think she's beginning to understand."

He looked down at the pork chop he was serving. "So. How are you going to find him?"

"I'm not. I gave the information to the police so they can set up a sting and catch him. We're going to let them handle it."

Dean held his breath as something shot through him. Not anger, exactly, but this sense that letting the police handle it wasn't enough. They'd set up a drug bust, arrest him for selling, and he'd get a slap on the wrist for being a drug dealer. But he was so much more. He was the reason Mandy had fallen so far. He could still vividly recall Alexa's voice as she explained what certified clean meant and what that implied. He fisted his hand so tightly around the knife he was holding, his knuckles turned white and started to ache.

"Dean," Alexa called, pulling him from his rage.

He looked over his shoulder at her.

"The police are going to handle it. They'll do a thorough investigation based on the information I gave them. They know to dig deeper than a few bags of weed."

Swallowing, he forced himself to nod. "Good. I'm glad." Turning, skillet in hand, he dropped a chop on each plate and then served mashed potatoes and fresh green beans. He'd gone all out for his first show of domesticity for Alexa. For some reason, showing her he could take care of her was important to him. He wanted her to know she could count on him.

The same way he needed to prove to Mandy that she could count on him.

As Alexa leaned forward and inhaled the scents rising from her plate, moaning her appreciation, Dean glanced at her bags on the sofa. He knew from experience she wrote everything in the little notebook she kept in her briefcase. The one she had used to make notes for Mandy's case had a red cover. He'd memorized the way the cardstock cover had frayed at the edge from the way Alexa ran her finger over it while thinking.

The notebooks she used were cheap when bought in bulk, but the contents were invaluable. He'd learned that, too, but until that moment, he hadn't realized just how invaluable. The information Mandy had given to Alexa was inside, jotted down in neat print with the most important bits underlined twice.

Taking a breath, he smiled at the woman complimenting his culinary skills. "Mom taught me to cook before I went to college so I wouldn't be forced to live on pasta and pizza. I still did," he said with a shrug, "but at least I could impress the girls if I needed to."

Alexa gave him a brilliant smile. "Ahh. I see. How many other girls have fallen victim to your fancy cooking?"

"None. I couldn't stop being a dork long enough to get them to my kitchen."

She giggled. "Good thing dork is the new stud."

"Good thing." Carrying their plates, he led her to the dining room. He set their plates down and grabbed the wine to fill their glasses as she took a seat. "I think I owe you a little romance, don't you?"

"I don't know about owing me, but I certainly am not complaining."

With the wine poured and the candles lit, he sat and grabbed her hand. "She was doing okay? Really?"

"As well as could be expected. She's angry and bitter and a little acidic, but physically, she's okay. She's going to get through this. Thanks to you and your determination to help her." Putting her palm to his cheek, she caressed his face. "You have done everything you can to save her."

He let a flat laugh rise from his throat. "I hear a *but* coming at the tail end of that."

"But she has to save herself now. She has to work the program and fight to stay sober once she leaves it. If she gets out of rehab and chooses to get high again, that's her choice. Her failure. Not yours. Okay?"

He let her words sink in before nodding. "Yeah." Taking a deep breath, he pushed it and some of his guilt out with it. "Let's eat before the neighborhood is overtaken by ghouls."

She enthusiastically dug into her dinner, groaning her appreciation. Dean suspected her excitement over the meal was her way of distracting him, but it didn't work. Nor did her stories of Halloweens past. Usually he was enthralled by her stories; he loved learning about her, especially when her eyes lit with happiness from days long gone. Tonight, however, her story of dressing up like the ass end of a unicorn while Lanie got to be the head barely registered in his ears.

She might be convinced that he'd done everything he could to help Mandy, but he wasn't. So long as the bastards who'd turned her into a prostitute were out there, he hadn't done nearly enough. He did his best to laugh when Alexa did and nod when she paused and keep his mouth full of pork and potato so he didn't have to say much, but when she finished eating, she sat back and frowned at him.

"Dean. Talk to me. What are you thinking?"

He pushed his plate back and rested his forearms on the table. "What you said...about Mandy having to choose to stay sober once she's out of rehab." He exhaled heavily. "This isn't over, is it?"

She shook her head. "It may never be over, honey. She's got a long road ahead of her, and she's going to have to be very careful of the path she takes."

"For some reason I thought this would end once she got clean."

Resting her hand on his forearm, she whispered, "This is just the beginning."

Dean glanced at his watch. "We better get this cleaned up so I can change into my costume." Leaning to her, he kissed her lips. "This is our first holiday together. I don't want to dwell on Mandy's problems."

The bright smile that crossed Alexa's face was enough

to lift his spirits from the darkness. "I hadn't thought of it that way. Our first holiday together. I like that." She batted his hand away when he reached for her plate. "I'll take care of this. You go change. I want to get a few pictures before kids start showing up."

He left her to clear the table as he rushed into his room and put on the costume he'd put together. He was buttoning up his black shirt when she walked in and dropped her bags on his bed.

"I brought makeup. The undead don't have such nice tans." Taking his hand, she pulled him into the bathroom and pried the top off a bottle before using a sponge to dab the pale color over his forehead, nose, and cheeks. Then she focused on his forehead again. When she stepped aside, his reflection was like hers—pale with an exaggerated widow's peak.

"We look amazing," she said, her smile still giddy.

"*You* are amazing." He pulled her against his side.

"Oh! I brought fake blood. Hang on." She disappeared for a few seconds before rushing back to his side and focusing intently as she squeezed a bit of cold liquid at the corners of his mouth and then did the same to hers.

Hearing her laugh at her handiwork made him smile, too. Other than that time he and his friends conspired to go as different members of *The Breakfast Club,* he'd never seen the appeal of having paired costumes, but looking at the woman at his side, both looking like bad recreations of Dracula, he got it. He seemed to be getting a lot of things these days that he'd missed in the past.

Her eyes widened when the doorbell chimed through the house. "Oh my gosh! They're starting already?"

"Go." Dean nodded toward the bathroom door. "I gotta get my shoes on. I'll be right there."

She darted from the room, rushing toward where the kids were waiting for their treats. He looked at his reflection, listening as her voice carried through the house, calling out for the kids to hang on one second. Though he knew he shouldn't, he headed straight for her briefcase and reached inside, his hearing tuned in to Alexa's movements on the other side of the house.

As she opened the door and cooed at the costumes, he pulled out the little red notebook. His fingers trembled as he flipped through the pages until he got to the last of the notes she'd made in her precise handwriting and, as he'd suspected, underlined twice.

Online. #d4dank. Any platform.

He snapped a picture and replaced the notebook. He slid his feet into his shoes and headed toward the door, where Alexa was handing out treats. He'd deal with Darrin the druggie later, but not too much later. If she'd already given this information to the cops, they'd be planning a bust.

Dean intended to get to the fucker first.

ONCE AGAIN, the reports Alexa needed to finish filling out took a back seat. This time to smiling at the photos on her phone. She'd taken about a dozen selfies with Dean in their vampire costumes, hamming it up. A few were sweet, like the one where he had his pale and bloodied lips pressed to her cheek. But most, like the one where he dipped her down and opened his mouth wide as if he were about to bite her neck, were hilarious.

"That's some smile," Rene said, coming into Alexa's office.

She turned her phone to share the image on the screen. "We had so much fun last night."

"I'm sure he's relieved to know his sister is off to rehab."

Alexa nodded. "The social worker called this morning to let him know she'd dropped Mandy off at a safe but undisclosed location. Dean can expect a few updates, but for the most part, this is out of his hands now. And I can tell you that I, for one, am so happy about that. He needs a break from all this stress."

Rene smiled. "You should take a weekend away. Just the two of you."

Alexa widened her eyes. "That is a fantastic idea. I love it. I'm going to talk to him about that tonight." Sitting back in her chair, she laughed slightly. "Is it crazy to be this happy when really I barely know the guy?"

"Maybe. Probably. But we live in an incredibly ugly world, Lex. Take your happiness where you can find it."

"Well. That's gloomy."

"That's realistic."

Again, Rene seemed to put off an air of stress and depression that wasn't like her. "Everything okay with you?" Alexa asked.

"This case I'm working on—"

"Not your case. *You.*"

"I'm fine."

"You haven't been fine in the year that I've known you."

Rene smiled. "That's nice." Dropping into the seat across from Alexa, she grabbed the reports. "What about you? You've been working on these for days. You're usually more efficient than this."

"Well...I'm having sex now." She waited for Rene's reaction, smiling when the other woman lifted a brow in surprise. "I was working on these the other day when Holly distracted me with alcohol. Yesterday I spent the morning prying information out of Mandy, the afternoon giving the information to the police, and the evening handing out candy. I'll get them done today."

"Did she actually give you any information?"

"Yeah. Surprisingly, she did. She found this guy online. Social media at its finest." Grabbing her notebook, she flipped through the pages. "A hashtag. That's all it took for her to..."

"What?"

Alexa touched the smudge of pale makeup. The makeup she'd used to cover Dean's tan. "The page with my notes on how to find the dealer who lured Mandy in has costume makeup all over it." She eyed her teammate. "There's only one person who could have—*would* have— looked at it."

"Dean."

"Dean."

"Get him on the phone before he does something stupid," Rene warned.

Alexa forcefully tapped her cell phone screen but wasn't surprised when her call went straight to voice mail. She was, however, even more alarmed. Her calls never went straight to voice mail. Dean always answered. "You call me the moment you get this," she stated angrily. Closing her eyes, she swallowed and forced her voice to soften. "Dean. Let the police handle this dealer. Please.

Call me." She gnawed at her lip for a moment before meeting Rene's gaze. "He is not a fighter. He's not equipped to confront this kind of criminal."

"Do you really think he would?"

Alexa closed her eyes, recalling the moment he'd stood in his kitchen, looking so angry as he clutched a knife in his hand as she explained she'd handed the matter to the police. He wasn't angry at her; she hadn't been concerned about that. She hadn't even been concerned that he'd do something this stupid. She'd been more concerned about the anger eating away at him and what that would do to his mental health. Guilt had a way of taking root and making the family members of survivors blame themselves. She didn't want that for him, not when he'd done so much to help Mandy.

She should have known. She should have seen through his anger to the real issue. She should have realized he wanted revenge for what his sister had been through. This wasn't a schoolyard fight, and this wasn't a bully he was going up against.

Alexa didn't know with any certainty that Darrin was a hardened gun-carrying criminal, but she highly doubted this man was a hippie growing pot in his basement and selling it to pay his rent. She suspected Darrin was just one part of a well-oiled, big-money machine. He was just the first step on a long path that led innocent young women from dabbling in drugs to being hardcore addicts willing to sell their bodies for their next hit.

No, this was no petty crime being committed here.

And Dean was nowhere near trained enough to deal with what he would face if he tried to confront the people running a human trafficking ring.

Rushing through her door, she screamed, "Sam! I need you!"

She reached Sam's desk, ignoring the questions of her teammate as to what was going on. Skidding to a stop in front of Sam, she demanded, "I need you to hack into Dean's social media. I think he set up a meeting with Mandy's dealer."

"Jesus," Holly breathed from her side.

Alexa hadn't even seen Holly approach. "The notes from my meeting with Mandy are covered in makeup. The makeup I put on him for Halloween."

"Maybe it's yours," Holly suggested.

"I haven't opened those notes since leaving the jail. He had to have read them."

Sam started pecking away at her keyboard. "You're going to have to give me some time, Lex. I can't just walk in."

"Are you sure?" Holly pressed.

"Track his cell phone," Rene suggested. "That'll be faster, right?"

Sam continued clicking. "Only if he has it on. Phone number?"

Alexa opened her phone and found his contact information before rattling it off.

An arm—she didn't know whose—wrapped around her shoulders, and she nearly crumbled at the thought that she'd been so careless. Reason one thousand and one why she shouldn't have gotten involved with a client. He never would have gotten access to this information if she hadn't been in such a hurry to get to him, to be with him, to go about their evening like everything was perfectly fine. Nothing was fine. He'd been raging about his sister's disappearance, about the abuse she'd faced, about the lack of care this man had for her well-being. And Alexa had dangled the man right in front of Dean's face.

"Got him," Sam said. "He's on the west side. Still moving."

"Let's go get him," Holly said. They didn't head for the front door, though. They all headed for their offices— their weapons. No one was going to say it, but they all knew Dean could be walking into a really bad situation.

The code Mandy had given them could have been a tip-off for Darrin. Using the hashtag could have been a warning to the dealer. This was why Alexa had handed the case to the police. This was why she was letting *them* handle taking Darrin down.

Damn it. If Dean got out of this unscathed, she was going to beat some sense into his rock-hard skull. With a gun on one hip and pepper spray on the other, Alexa met Holly and Rene in the lobby.

"I'll call you from the car," Holly said to Sam. "Don't take your eyes off him until you hear from us."

"Should I call the cops?" Sam asked.

"We don't know anything yet," Rene answered. "He may just be making a coffee run."

Not likely. There was a coffee shop two blocks from his house that had the medium roast he preferred. He was over ten miles away. And not answering his phone.

"Try him again," Holly suggested as she started her car.

Alexa slammed the passenger door shut and grabbed her seat belt with one hand, all while tapping her phone with the other. Holly had peeled out of her parking spot and headed toward the west side of town before Alexa gave up. "He's still not answering. Damn him."

She let out a heavy breath as she looked out the window, her mind filling with worry.

"This isn't your fault," Rene offered from the back seat, seeming to know what Alexa was thinking.

"I should have locked my bag in the trunk before I went in."

"You don't know for certain he looked at your notes."

"I do," she stated. "I saw his face when I told him I'd turned this over to the cops. He wanted revenge, not justice."

"You can't blame him," Rene said. "Not really."

"We're not in the business of revenge," Holly reminded her.

"We're not. But the big brother of a girl who's been sold like meat on the market for the last few months has the right to be."

Alexa watched Holly cast a disapproving frown at Rene.

"I should have known better," Alexa said, bringing the

focus back to her lapse in judgment. She preferred that over the exchange of words between her teammates that was about to erupt. Holly was a straight-arrow, by-the-law type. Rene was a bit more flexible at times. She understood the human emotion behind actions better than Holly.

But Alexa wasn't interested in either take on the issue. She just wanted to get to Dean and make sure he was safe.

Maybe Rene was right. Maybe he was out running errands and all this drama was for naught. But somehow she didn't believe that. "Call Sam," she said by means of offering another distraction.

Sam's voice came over the speaker. "He's still on the move." She rattled off the cross streets closest to his location as Alexa tried to call him again.

This time when he didn't answer, Alexa texted him. *Call me. Now.* She held her phone, staring at the screen. No response.

Dean. Do not put yourself in danger. That won't help Mandy.

Her phone remained silent. Damn it.

DEAN HAD SILENCED HIS PHONE FOR A REASON. As they'd sipped coffee at the kitchen counter, he'd asked Alexa what was on her agenda for the day. She'd smiled as she answered she had to finish the report on Mandy's case and then planned to take the afternoon off. She'd asked if he wanted to meet for a late lunch.

He'd lied. He hated it, but he'd lied. He said he couldn't because he had to catch up on a huge project. He took his lie another step and suggested, without saying it, that he wouldn't see her until the next day.

She hadn't seemed offended. It wasn't like they were living together or were in a serious relationship. She seemed to take his unspoken suggestion in stride, noting that her grandmother had been complaining about how much time had passed since the last time Alexa had sat with her through dinner. That led Alexa to invite him to meet the woman whose cooking he had grown to adore.

The conversation flowed like so many before—easy and with a familiarity that reminded him how lucky he was to have found her. After he'd kissed her and walked her to the door, Dean had taken his betrayal of her trust to the next level.

He'd dropped into his office chair, turned on his computer, and opened his Internet browser. Then he'd made contact with Mandy's drug dealer. By the time he'd showered and dressed, the bastard had replied, asking what he was interested in. Dean, God forgive him, had used the only drug-buying story he could think of—he'd told the man that his mother was suffering from the side effects of chemotherapy and the doctor refused to give her medicinal marijuana. He didn't know what he needed, or how much, or anything, really. He just knew he needed something to help his poor, sick mother.

Dean felt queasy using his mother's illness like that, but he really didn't know what else to say. He didn't know how to buy drugs any more now than he had when his mother really had needed the pot to take the edge off her symptoms. The likelihood of the man meeting him if he'd pointed out that he just wanted to bash his face in for prostituting his sister wasn't very high. So he'd used his mom and spent the drive to meet Darrin to convince himself that she would approve.

Darrin had bought it. He offered his sympathies and told Dean he had something to help. Dean played up his desperation, begging to meet the man as soon as possible. Then paced and tried to tell himself how stupid this was for the next two hours. Finally, when it was time to leave to meet Darrin, Dean looked at his phone, considering that he should call Alexa and confess everything.

But then he thought about Mandy and all she'd been through and turned the sound off on his phone.

He cared about Alexa—so much so that it scared him if he spent too much time thinking about how little he knew about her—but he'd let her fight his fight long enough. He'd needed her help to find Mandy. It was up to him to avenge what had been done to her. He didn't have to guess what Alexa would say to that. Hell, she'd already said it. She'd warned him more than once the day before to let the police handle things now. Mandy was safe, and Alexa thought that was what Dean should focus on. But he couldn't.

He wasn't a violent guy, but this piece of shit had

abused his sister, and Dean wasn't just going to walk away from that. He just hoped Alexa would bail his ass out of jail when he got done giving Darrin a taste of what the prick deserved.

Pulling into the mall parking lot, Dean circled, following the signs to where Darrin had suggested they meet. One of the bigger stores in the building had a huge parking lot. Dean needed to go to the row directly aligned with the main entrance of the store and park as far from the building as he could. From there, he just needed to sit and wait for Darrin.

"This is stupid," he whispered to himself. But then he pictured Mandy, stoned and posing in her underwear for a photo that was posted online. A post that noted she was "certified clean" so men would pay more to have sex with her. "Fucking prick," he said angrily as his fury reignited. He clenched the steering wheel, ground his teeth, and exhaled a harsh breath, tapping into the rage that had fueled him for the last few months.

Parking his car where Darrin had told him, Dean unbuckled and grabbed his phone. He'd missed four calls from Alexa and about half a dozen texts, each one begging him not to do exactly what he was doing.

He started to reply, but what was he going to say? That he was sorry? He wasn't. He hated that he'd taken her notes without telling her, he hated that he hadn't been honest with her about his intentions, but he wasn't sorry about what he was doing. This son of a bitch deserved to have his ass kicked for what he'd done to Mandy and who knew how many other young women like her. He deserved to have to pay for what he'd done to the women; not just selling them drugs but breaking them down to the point that they were helpless.

Without a single way to justify what he'd done and was about to do, he tossed his phone aside, accepting that he'd have to reconcile with her later. He thought she'd understand, was certain that he could convince her he'd done what he had to, but he had to admit he was worried that she'd never trust him completely again. Trust was important to her. She'd never said as much, but he had learned that about her just from being with her. He had little doubt that she was feeling betrayed at the moment.

Raking his hand over his hair, he felt doubt creep in on him again. The one and only time he'd gotten into a fist-fight was with Jared Conner, a basketball player on the high school team who had called Dean's then-girlfriend a bitch. He'd only said that because the girl turned him in for cheating off her history exam.

One thing Dean had little tolerance for was men demeaning women. He guessed that stemmed back to his father and the way he treated his throwaway family. Dean's mom had never been good enough according to his dad—she was too fat, too thin, too dressed up, not dressed up enough. Nothing she had done was ever right. Hearing that growing up had left Dean sensitive to men picking on women. It tripped a trigger in him, and when his girlfriend had run to him crying, he'd stormed off to the gym and punched Jared Conner right in the jaw.

Then Dean had been thrown flat on his back and the wind was knocked out of him. The rest of the fight was a blur—he didn't remember much—but he did know that even after a week's suspension, when he returned to school, the player had the remnants of a black eye and a busted lip. And he never called Dean's girlfriend a derogatory name again.

This wasn't exactly the same, he knew that. But the one good thing he had gotten from his father was just enough stubbornness to not back down even when he knew what he was doing was dumb. Then again, maybe that wasn't a good trait.

A black sedan with tinted windows parked next to him, and the tension in Dean's stomach knotted. No backing out now. Fisting his hands several times and exhaling all his breath, he braced himself for the confrontation about to take place. Climbing from his car, he forced a smile as Darrin rounded the trunk of his car and held his hand out.

They were supposed to act like friends. That was what Darrin had said in his message. *Cameras are everywhere,* he'd warned Dean.

Gotta make it look like we're buds, okay?

Buds. Yeah. Okay.

The man's smile was friendly, warm, and welcoming. On the surface, he had the kind of face that would make him approachable in a bar. The kind of guy someone looking for a beer and a little surface chat would sit next to. He didn't seem threatening or intimidating in any way.

He was clean-cut but without the hard line of looking like a jock or cocky. He just looked like a normal, confident guy.

No wonder Mandy never had any red flags going off in her mind. Dean wouldn't either if he didn't know the truth. This man was the perfect bait for an innocent young girl.

Dean held Darrin's hand when he started to lean back. Clutching the other man's shoulder, he held him close. Darrin narrowed his eyes at him, clearly questioning the actions.

Dean stared into his eyes as his adrenaline flared and anger filled his veins. "Do you ever feel guilty for what you've done?" he asked, his voice echoing through his ears with a hard edge that he'd never heard come from his lips before.

"For selling pot?" Darrin asked.

"For entrapping women in a world of drugs and prostitution."

Darrin's breath caught and denial clearly played on his lips, but then he smirked. "No. Never. Because they get exactly what they ask for and they *love* me for it."

Like a lit fuse, Dean exploded. He did some kung fu move he didn't even know he held in his repertoire, something he'd probably seen in a movie. He took a step back, still holding Darrin and attempted to turn the man into a headlock so he could pound his fucking face in.

Dean, however, wasn't nearly as successful as a fictional superhero with the move. He twisted Darrin's upper torso, but before he could pin the man to his side, he felt the crush of a fist to his ribcage. His breath rushed from him and he grunted with surprise, but he didn't let go. He wasn't about to let go. He swung his fist, making contact, but probably even less effectively than the twist-hold-punch move he'd attempted.

Darrin fought back, landing another hit to Dean's side. The pain shot through him this time, and he instinctively eased his hold. Shoving Dean back, he chuckled mockingly.

"Let me guess," he taunted. "You must be Mandy's brother. She told me about you. How worthless you are. How you didn't care about her." He swung as Dean was standing, catching his breath, and his fist hit Dean's jaw.

That hurt. Bad. His teeth ground against each other, but he held his ground. He swung as well, landing a hit square against Darrin's nose. The man grunted, grabbed the wound, and then shook it off. Blood oozed out of his nostrils, but he seemed unfazed. He smiled that asshole smile of his before spitting.

"It's your fault, you know," Darrin taunted. "She needed the drugs to escape you."

Grunting, Dean lurched forward, tackling Darrin around the chest. They landed on the ground, skidding a few inches as Dean leaned back to slam his fist into Darrin's lying face. He didn't get a chance. Darrin clung to him and rolled him over, taking the advantage. Dean took three solid punches to the face before Darrin stood, pulling him with him.

Shaking Dean, Darrin held his gaze. "Did she send you? Huh? That little bitch send you to settle a score?" Dropping his hold on Dean, he shoved. "She'll be back. She's weak. Like you. She'll be back. And when she comes crawling to me," he said, smiling with blood in his teeth, "I'll put her to good use while she's on her knees."

Dean actually felt something inside him snap. He embraced a level of insanity that would have scared a normal person. Screaming like a maniac, he attacked. Dean's fist met Darrin's flesh; he tightened his fingers around Darrin's neck. He slammed the dealer's head forward, cracking his own skull against that fucker's so hard that Dean saw stars. He didn't care. He wasn't bothered by the pain. He tightened his hold as Darrin gagged. He would kill him before he let him touch Mandy again. He would choke the life out of this bastard and never regret it. Never.

Darrin's eyes rolled back, and he seemed to be growing weaker when someone grabbed Dean's shoulders. He didn't let go. In fact, he squeezed Darrin's neck tighter.

"Enough!" Alexa screamed, and he finally heard her. "Dean! Enough."

He didn't relent until she wrapped her arm around his throat and dragged him away, gagging and resisting with each inch. She practically tossed him aside, and he landed on the hard parking lot, glaring up at her. He wasn't angry at her; he was pissed she'd shown up before he could finish what he'd started.

"He isn't worth it," she stated. "He *isn't* worth it!"

"He destroyed her," he justified.

"And killing him will destroy you." Her furious eyes softened. "Let the police handle it."

Dean sagged, breathless and suddenly exhausted.

"Stay down," someone ordered.

Dean looked beyond Alexa in time to see Darrin get to his feet and lurch. He reached up, ready to shove Alexa aside so she wasn't between him and the bastard he'd tried to choke to death, but she stepped forward.

Where his kung fu moves had failed, hers were on point. She didn't even grunt as she slammed her hand against Darrin's chest to knock him back, twisted his arm, and pushed him to his knees. "Do you want me to let him finish you off?" she screamed in Darrin's ear. "I'll break your fucking arms and let him at you. You bastard."

Darrin screamed out in obvious pain before promising not to move again. Standing up, Alexa shook her head at Dean. "Do you know what you've done?"

He didn't answer. He'd known what he was doing was stupid, but for the first time he felt real shame for his actions.

Rene moved to stand guard over Darrin as Alexa stood over Dean. She shook her head at him again. "Who swung first?"

Dean thought for a moment. "I did."

"That's great. Now he can press assault charges against you. Do you realize that?" She gestured around them. "The mall security cameras got it all on tape, Dean.

He has all the evidence he needs to put you in jail. And he walks."

"He has drugs on him. He came here to sell me drugs."

"Oh, so a drug deal gone bad. That defense really isn't in your favor."

Dean exhaled harshly. "He sold my sister."

"You came here with the intent of assaulting him." Alexa kneeled down and held his gaze. "Make a deal with him. You won't go to the cops if he doesn't."

"No."

"Make a deal with him so you both walk."

"He's not walking."

She whispered, "He'll get a slap on the wrist and disappear before the cops can nail him for anything more than distribution. Let him go so they can nail him on something bigger. Dean," she whispered harshly. "Let him go."

He looked at the son of a bitch and noticed Rene having a heated discussion with him, too. Probably the same context. Walk away before anyone gets in trouble for something bigger. Darrin looked across the lot. Dean met his gaze and knew agreeing to turn his back on the man was the only way to catch him in the end.

ALEXA DIDN'T FEEL A BIT GUILTY WHEN DEAN winced in pain. She pressed the ice pack against his bruised and swollen eye and took pleasure in knowing the pressure hurt. That was what he deserved. The idiot.

She'd taken him home while Rene and Holly followed. Rene dropped his car off in the driveway, and then Holly took them back to the office, leaving Alexa to clean up the mess Dean had created.

"He could have killed you," she snapped, no longer able to hold in her anger.

"I know."

"He could have had a knife or a gun, and what did you have, Dean?"

"I was winning the fight when you showed up."

His reasoning didn't appease her. In fact, his sarcasm ignited her temper, and she realized how her mother must have felt when Alexa was a defiant teen, snapping back when she should have just kept her mouth shut. Pressing the ice pack harder against his face, she narrowed her eyes. "Is that what you call it? What would you have done if you had killed him? Gone to prison. For what?"

The light of amusement in his eyes faded. "I'm sorry."

"Don't apologize to me," she bit back. "You're the one who would have done time. You'd just better hope that he sticks to the agreement and doesn't go to the cops."

"He has a lot more to lose than I do."

She sighed. "Do you know how much more difficult it's going to be to nail him? He's going to be very careful going forward."

"No, he won't." Dean pulled his face back and took the pack from her hand. "He's too cocky to think that he could get caught. He was gloating about what he does.

He's proud of himself. He'll slip up, and now that we know who he is, someone will catch him."

Alexa heaved another frustrated breath. She had called the officer she'd spoken with the day before, the one who had taken her information on Darrin, and given him the make, model, and plate on his car...after letting him know that her client had intervened and likely tipped the criminal off that he was being looked into. She'd passed that bit of information along while giving Dean a disapproving side-eye that had caused him to moan and roll his head back.

She filled a glass of water and slid it to him so he could take the aspirin he'd gotten from the bathroom while she'd wrapped an ice pack in a towel. "You snooped through my bag."

He lowered his gaze and nodded. "I did. For that, I really am sorry. I just... What would you do?" Meeting her eyes, he pleaded, "If you found the man who hurt your sister, what would you do?"

Alexa swallowed as she put herself in his shoes. "I'd hunt him down and gut him like a fish."

He nodded, one solitary but confident nod, before taking the pills that would help ease the ache she was certain he was feeling.

"I've lost a lot of people in my life, Dean. I can't lose anyone else. I won't survive it." She blinked, surprised by her own words. But there it was, her darkest fear voiced. "I don't care if this thing between us is new. It's real. I feel it my soul. We were supposed to find each other. I wouldn't survive losing you."

His eyes saddened, as if he finally realized the depth of his mistake. "I'm sorry. I didn't mean..." He pushed himself up, rounded the counter, and pulled her into his arms. "I didn't mean to scare you."

Wrapping her arms around him, she inhaled his scent deep into her, memorizing his warmth and his body against hers. After her father died, she'd started writing little moments like these to her memory so she could reflect on them later. She'd never taken the time to soak in her sister like this, or her father. But she had her mami, abuela, and all the HEARTS tucked away in her heart. And now she had Dean there.

Easing his hold on her, he leaned back and brushed his hand over her hair. "I feel it, too. That we're here for a reason. I think I've been looking for you my entire life."

Smiling, she brushed her hand over his beard, careful of the wounds. But then she wiped the grin from her face. "If you ever ignore my calls again, I'll kick your ass, and I'll do a much better job than was done today. Understand?"

"I understand." Cupping her head, he pulled her closer. "I love you."

Alexa's breath caught. "Dean," she whispered. "Don't say that unless—"

"You say, 'I love you, too.'"

Brushing her hand over his hair, she stared into his eyes, needing to see the truth there the way she could so easily see the love in her papi's eyes when he looked at her mother. There, she saw the deep affection in his eyes she'd needed to see. Pressing her mouth to his, she kissed him hard. "I love you, too." Breaking the connection, she nabbed the ice pack and pressed it to his face. "But I still think you're an idiot."

The End

CONTINUE HEARTS SERIES WITH SECRET HEARTS

The Women of HEARTS Series Book Four

U.S. Marshal Quinn Stanton took in the scene at a so-called federal safe house. Blood spatter covered nearly every surface of the living room. The couple he and his team had been protecting had clearly been tortured prior to being killed. Richard Bantam's stomach had been slit open and his innards placed on his chest. *Disemboweled.* The method of choice for killing snitches in the circles Richard had run in for decades. Sharon, his wife, used to talk a mile a minute. Now her tongue was gone and her throat slit. Their deaths had been violent and painful. Even more—the grisly killings would send a message to anyone else who might be thinking about talking to the feds.

The marshals were responsible for keeping witnesses safe until they could testify and relocate with new identities. In exchange for their cooperation catching bigger criminals, the witnesses' past sins were forgiven and the government helped them start over.

Quinn had been with the agency for almost a decade now. This was the first time one of his witnesses had been murdered in all those years.

This was bad. On so many levels.

Richard had laundered money for the better part of twenty years for a Columbian crime organization based in New York. His wife had bragged about their ability to keep the IRS off their trail a little too loudly, which led to a long federal investigation of the Bantams and their connection to the ring. Thanks to Sharon's big mouth, the feds got the information they needed and in exchanged offered the family a cozy new life via the Witness Security Program. WITSEC was supposed to keep them safe. But soon after the family was reborn in a new city with new names, Quinn started to suspect they weren't as safe as they should have been. He insisted on staying with the family long after the witnesses would normally have been passed off to local marshals. Quinn's gut had told him to keep close. Too bad that instinct hadn't been enough to keep them alive.

Just last week, he'd asked that the family be trans-ferred to the WITSEC Operations Center where they could be better protected. His request had been denied. Other than a hunch, Quinn didn't have proof to substan-tiate his concerns. Another relocation would have been expensive and inconvenient for all involved. He felt sick to his stomach, but not because of the gory crime scene. The only way the Bantams could have been found and murdered was if his gut had been right. Someone with inside information was responsible for this.

Now the Bantams were sprawled across the living room of their new home as blood dried on the walls, the ceiling fan, and soaked into the gray shag carpet.

Not all the Bantams were accounted for, however.

"Where's Logan?" Quinn asked. The six-year-old boy who cried every night because he missed his old room and his toys and his friends was not among the fatalities—his parents—in the living room.

"We haven't found him," Frank Strickland said. "They probably took him."

Quinn didn't blink, didn't jolt, but he did hold his breath for a second. His coworker came to that conclusion with as much emotion as he'd order a cup of coffee. Quinn knew being hardened against violence was part of the job, but Frank's lack of compassion was a red flag that Quinn tucked away in the back of his mind with the rest of the flags he'd been collecting over the last few weeks.

Keith Wilson, another member of Quinn's team, exhaled loudly. "We'll get a team looking for the boy. If he isn't dead, he'll be for sale soon."

Just like his gut had told him the Bantams were in danger, Quinn's gut told him Logan wasn't about to be put on the Black Market. He always listened to his gut.

His old team leader had pounded into their heads that they listen to their instincts. She said they didn't have to believe in karma or God or anything else, but they damned well better believe what their guts told them. Quinn did. He'd known something bad was going to happen. He'd tried to warn his supervisors. Nobody had listened.

Quinn hoped Logan had listened. He hoped the kid heard every word Quinn had told him when he'd pulled him aside and showed him where to hide if something went down.

Slipping away from the team he'd grown suspicious of, Quinn moved down the hallway of the contemporary ranch house to Logan's bedroom. The room was decked out in a race car theme that the little boy had confided in Quinn that he hated. Looking around the room, Quinn's heart started beating faster. The red racecar-shaped bed had been flipped over and the clothes from the closet had been tossed on the floor. Whoever had broken in had looked for the boy. They'd intended to kill him, too.

Quinn looked down the hallway, verifying he hadn't been followed, before easing the bedroom door shut. Moving to the window, he slid the glass pane open and popped the screen. Poking his head out, he checked that the small grassy area was clear. A week ago, when his suspicions grew into real concern, he'd crept around the back of the house and loosened three boards in the wooden privacy fence. Removing those boards would leave a big enough hole that a grown man and a little boy could escape in a hurry.

Crossing the room in three long strides, Quinn aimed his flashlight toward the ceiling of the closet. He whispered the code phrase Logan had chosen: "Race cars suck."

A moment later, Logan peered out from the top of the shelves. His eyes were wide and his lip trembled. Quinn pressed his finger to his lips to signal Logan to be quiet, and then he gestured for the boy to come out of hiding.

Logan climbed down the shelves and took Quinn's hand, without a word. Quinn glanced through the window and confirmed the backyard was still empty. Thankfully, the agents were still focused on the bloody scene in the living room. He slid the glass open, popped the screen, and lifted Logan through the window. After Quinn set the boy outside, he climbed from the window too. Once safely on the grass outside in the yard, he pulled the window closed behind them and replaced the screen so they didn't tip anyone off.

Quinn guided the boy through the loose boards and then followed him. In the alley, Quinn hefted Logan onto his back and hooked his arms around the kid's thin legs. Logan clung to him, hugging tight, as Quinn ran off into the night.

ALSO BY MARCI BOLDEN

STONEHILL SERIES:

The Road Leads Back

Friends Without Benefits

The Forgotten Path

Jessica's Wish

This Old Cafe

Forever Yours

THE WOMEN OF HEARTS SERIES:

Hidden Hearts

Burning Hearts

Stolen Hearts

Secret Hearts

OTHER TITLES:

California Can Wait

Seducing Kate

A Life Without Water

As a teen, Marci Bolden skipped over young adult books and jumped right into reading romance novels. She never left.

Marci lives in the Midwest with her husband, kiddos, and numerous rescue pets. If she had an ounce of willpower, Marci would embrace healthy living, but until cupcakes and wine are no longer available at the local market, she will appease her guilt by reading self-help books and promising to join a gym "soon."

Visit her here:
www.marcibolden.com

 facebook.com/MarciBoldenAuthor

 twitter.com/BoldenMarci

 instagram.com/marciboldenauthor

CPSIA information can be obtained
at www.ICGtesting.com
Printed in the USA
LVHW090010151019
634223LV00001B/27/P